He opened another cabinet, a larger one and lifted the chainsaw out, laying it on the work bench. It was heavy, fifteen pounds, but Edward hardly noticed its bulk as he held it before him, studying the sixteen-inch blade, the vicious hooks set in every other link of the chain which ran around the polished metal. It was a McCulloch, a powerful tool, able to cut through wood as thick as forty inches at a stroke. He had even seen it plough through metal. He didn't have much use for it but, just like all the other equipment and tools he owned, he kept it oiled and in perfect working order. He lifted it once more, running a hand over the savage, barbed chain, careful not to cut himself on the teeth . . .

COME THE NIGHT

NIGHT

Nick Blake

A STAR BOOK
published by
the Paperback Division of
W.H. Allen & Co. PLC

A Star Book
Published in 1985
by the Paperback Division of
W.H. Allen & Co. PLC
44 Hill Street, London W1X 8LB

First published in Great Britain by the Paperback Division of
W.H. Allen & Co. PLC, 1984, under the title of *Chainsaw Terror*

Copyright © Nick Blake, 1984

Printed in Great Britain by
Hunt Barnard Printing Ltd, Aylesbury, Bucks.

ISBN 0 352 31753 1

For MB
who unlocked the toolbox

COME THE NIGHT

Prologue

April 21st, 1978:

The tool bag made a dull metallic clanging sound as it was dropped and the top popped open to reveal the wicked curved edge of a hatchet. The blade was sticky with oil and there were pieces of fluff and wood chippings stuck to it.

Ralph Briggs stooped wearily and replaced the hatchet, checking the fastening on the bag, tugging on the crinkled leather and making a mental note to replace the hold-all as soon as he could. He didn't want his tools falling out all over the place next time he went out. The bag was nearly as old as Briggs himself, its once supple sheen now dull and wrinkled with the passage of time, much like the man's own face. There were deep lines across his forehead and around his eyes but the creases which flared up from his eye corners were not the laugh-lines possessed by so many others. These deep indentations were the result of the perpetual frown which he wore. A mask which rarely slipped when he was at home and one which could only grudgingly be removed for the benefit of customers.

Ralph Briggs had been a carpenter for the past twenty-six years. Taught everything he knew by his father, he had continued with the business which his father had fought so hard to build up. Briggs himself had seen it expand over the years. He had begun by doing jobs for people in the neighbourhood and the work had gradually escalated until he was forced to think of taking on extra help. But Ralph Briggs preferred not to trust his work to anyone else so he slogged away alone, working until late most nights. Indeed, for the amount of time he saw his family, he might as well have been a lodger in their large, eight-roomed house in

Kilburn. He was like a stranger who arrived only to eat his meals in the mornings and evenings, speaking a few cursory words to his family and receiving the type of reaction from them which might usually have been reserved for an intruder, not a father and husband. But he had given them all he could. There just never seemed to be the time. He never took holidays and, even if he did, they were usually spent down in the cellar where his vast horde of tools was kept and where he could saw and hammer. And create.

Ralph Briggs was proud of his skills and he had used them to good effect over the years. During one of his brief breaks he had put up partitions in many of the rooms, even allowing his son, Edward, who, at twenty-six, still lived at home, to help paint the finished articles. On another break, he had soundproofed the house. Despite the fact that it stood apart from the other dwellings around it, Briggs had still found the need to cut out all sounds of the outside world, as if the noise of other people annoyed him. And, indeed, that wasn't far from the truth. He was an unsociable man, uncomfortable in company, preferring to be alone as often as possible.

His son was the same. Edward had grown up to be very like his father both in character and also in attitude. Briggs hoped that his son would take over the business when he died or found that he could no longer manage the protracted and often backbreaking schedule which he worked.

Indeed, as Briggs looked at his watch and saw that it was barely six p.m., he sighed and ran a hand through his greying hair. He should have been working in a house nearby, putting on a new back door but the tenants had gone away unexpectedly and he had been forced to come home earlier than he had anticipated. He turned and wandered into the sitting room where he found his son sitting before the television.

Edward looked up and nodded a greeting which Briggs returned almost with effort.

'You're early,' said the younger man.

Briggs nodded and explained why.

'Where's Maureen?' he asked, reaching into the pocket of his overalls for the tin of tobacco which was always there. He took off the lid, which came free with a low sucking sound, and proceeded to roll himself a cigarette.

'She should be home soon,' Edward told him. 'She usually gets in around half past six.' He was referring to his sister, two years his junior, who worked for an insurance agency in South London and, like him, shared the house with her parents.

'And your mother?' asked Briggs, drawing on his fag.

'Upstairs,' Edward told him.

Briggs nodded again and walked through into the kitchen where he ran the cold tap for a moment then scooped a handful of water into his mouth, having put the roll-up on the draining board. He washed his hands, splashed his face with cold water then took a towel from the wooden rack which he himself had made and wiped the moisture away. Pushing the cigarette back into his mouth, he made his way back through the sitting room and up the stairs.

As he reached the landing he found the four doors before him all tightly closed. There was very little noise, the soundproofing of the house making everything even more hushed. It was like standing in a church. A few tarnished rays of sunlight found their way through the window to his right and he paused momentarily, watching as dust particles dipped and bobbed in the paling light, seemingly suspended in the burnished shafts.

Briggs crossed to the first door on his left, still listening for any sounds of movement from within. He pushed open the door.

For brief seconds, he caught sight of his own reflection in the large mirror which topped the antique dressing table in the far corner of the room. The face which stared back at him was one that showed puzzlement, even surprise.

Sheila Briggs looked up as he opened the door but did not stop what she was doing. She folded the dress carefully and laid it on top of the other clothes in the suitcase which was on the bed, its lid propped open. Indeed, she seemed not to

9

have noticed his presence for she merely turned to the wardrobe and took out another garment which she likewise folded and tucked away.

For long moments neither of them spoke. She carefully packing her case, he taking a last draw on his cigarette then nipping it out, dropping the butt into the pocket of his overalls.

'What are you doing?' he asked, still puzzled.

'What does it look like I'm doing?' she said, acidly. She reached into the wardrobe for a blouse. Sheila Briggs was forty-four, two years younger than her husband, but her looks and figure belied that age. Apart from a little too much weight around the hips and backside, she was an attractive, if somewhat stockily built woman and the sunlight, playing across her auburn hair made it look as though her head was ablaze. She barely looked at Briggs as she continued with her chore.

'I thought you were going to be late,' she told him. 'I hoped I might have been gone before you got back.'

'Gone? What the hell are you talking about?' he asked, taking a step into the room.

'I'm leaving, Ralph,' she said, flatly. 'Something I should have done years ago.' She placed another blouse in the case.

'Why?' he wanted to know.

She smiled bitterly.

'You really don't know do you?'

He took another step into the room and closed the door behind him.

'No I don't, why don't you try telling me,' he said, his voice a mixture of anger and surprise.

'Maybe if you'd been here more often this wouldn't have happened. You were never home long enough to see that our marriage was falling apart were you? All that mattered was your job. Not me, not the kids. You haven't had any time for them since they were born. I might as well have been on my own for all the help you were.'

'We never went short of anything. There was always money . . .'

She cut him short.

'There's more to marriage than money, Ralph,' she rasped. 'There's love, concern and understanding. Things that we've never had.' She paused for a moment. 'Have you ever loved me? I mean *really* loved me?'

'In my own way,' he said defensively.

'I used to love you once. When we were first married. But not anymore. How the hell can you love a man who you never see?' Her voice had risen in volume. 'We share this bed at nights but I might as well be sleeping with a corpse. Is there something wrong with me, Ralph? Why is it you haven't touched me in six years?' She paused. 'Or is it that there's something wrong with *you*?'

'So where do you think you're going then, once you leave here?' he demanded.

'Where I've been going for the last year,' she told him. 'To live with Ken.'

'Who the hell is Ken? And what are you talking about, seeing him for the last year?' He was flushed now, his anger bubbling up. 'Have you been seeing another man?'

'Yes.' She said it defiantly, no hint of regret. 'If you'd have bothered to look more closely in the beginning you might have avoided it.'

Outside the door, Edward listened intently, standing as close as he dare, glancing behind him to make sure that he could retreat to his own room swiftly if the need arose. He listened, dumb-struck, as they argued.

'And have you been sleeping with this bloody bloke too?' demanded Briggs, moving towards her now. For the first time, she felt her courage faltering.

'Yes I have,' she told him, finding new strength suddenly. 'And I'll tell you one thing, he's better than you ever

11

were. He made me feel like a woman not a bloody ornament.'

'You fucking whore,' rasped Briggs, his jaw set, the knot of muscles at one side pulsing angrily.

'I've had enough, Ralph,' she said, swallowing hard.

'And you think you're just going to walk out of here. Throw away twenty-seven years just like that? Wreck our marriage.'

'Oh, wake up for God's sake, our marriage isn't wrecked,' she yelled at him. 'It's dead. It's been dead for years. Dead and buried.'

He struck her hard across the face, knocking her onto the bed. She fell sideways, licking at the bloodied cleft in her lower lip. The blow dazed her but she managed to get to her feet.

'You bastard,' she murmured, touching the cut gently.

They eyed each other for long seconds, standing mere feet apart like two boxers, each waiting for the other to make a move.

'Is that your only answer,' she said, scornfully, touching her split lip once more. 'You think that knocking me about is going to solve the problem? It's over, Ralph. Everything between us is over. I don't think it really ever started.'

She reached for the suitcase but he grabbed her wrist and squeezed hard, his face set.

'You're not leaving this house,' he rasped.

'Let go of me,' she said, trying to pull away.

He kept his vice-like grip on her wrist, noticing that her hand was turning white.

'You're not leaving.'

She struck out at him with her free hand, her nails raking his face, drawing blood and the shock made him release her. Now it was his turn to see his own blood. His face darkened and he moved towards her again, this time striking her with a clenched fist. He felt the bones of her nose splinter under the impact and she fell back onto the bed once more, her limbs flopping about like a puppet with its wires cut but she clung to conciousness and, as he straddled her, pinning her down, she could see the anger in his eyes.

12

'You're not leaving this house,' he told her again.

Edward peered through the keyhole, watching them, mesmerised by the sight before him. He saw his father kneeling on Sheila's arms and her trying desperately to extricate herself.

She glared up at him, her head thrashing back and forth madly. She could smell the odour of stale sweat on him, the thick aroma of tobacco which seemed to coat his body and, each time he spoke, spittle flew from his mouth. He gripped her chin in one powerful hand, ignoring the blood which ran from her nostrils.

'You think you can walk out and make a fool of me?' he rasped.

She stopped struggling for a moment and met his gaze.

'You *are* a fool,' she told him. 'You're useless. Why do you think I found myself another man in the first place?'

He struck her again and she yelped in pain but, this time, she squirmed beneath him and brought one knee up. It thudded into his groin and he gasped, clutching at his genitals and swaying slightly. She clawed at his already bleeding cheek, pieces of skin coming away beneath her fingernails and, as he toppled to one side, she clambered to her feet and dashed for the door.

Outside, Edward took a step backwards.

But Sheila never reached the door. Briggs shot out a hand and succeeded in grasping her wrist. He tugged and she felt something in her shoulder tear. Then, using all his strength, he hurled her across the room. She crashed into the sideboard, her head snapping forward to connect with the mirror which promptly shattered, large heavy lumps of glass falling to the floor. There was an explosion of blood on her forehead as several of the smaller shards slashed open the skin and she went down in a heap, the crimson liquid flowing freely from the vicious rent which had opened up just above her hairline. Her auburn hair was swiftly matted by the thick blood and, as she rolled onto her back, she saw Briggs advancing towards her. He stooped to pick up a length of thick mirror about eighteen inches long, then, gripping it by the broad end of the wedge, he stood over her.

She screamed but, even if there had been anyone passing outside, they would not have heard her, the house's sound-proofing ensured that.

'You're not leaving this house,' he yelled at her, raising the shaft of crystal. 'You're not leaving *me*.'

He brought the length of mirror down with as much force as he could muster and, in one last desperate attempt to save herself, she raised a hand. The razor sharp point punctured her palm and erupted from the back of her hand and, as Briggs tore it free, the end broke off. Blood splashed the piece of glass and, for brief seconds, she could see her bloodied, terrified, reflection in the lump which he held.

She managed to get to her knees, other small pieces of shattered crystal from the broken mirror cutting her flesh as she moved.

Briggs struck at her again and, this time, the deadly shaft caught her in the side. It sliced effortlessly through the side of her left breast and a gout of blood erupted from the wound. He felt it strike something hard and realized that it must be her ribs. She fell forward, trying to crawl away, as if she were attempting to hide beneath the bed like a child might hide while playing a game. But this was no game.

'You can't leave me,' he shrieked and now the anger in his voice had almost turned to pity. He brought the length of mirror down and buried it just beneath her right shoulder blade. It punctured a lung as he put all his weight behind it and there was a loud hissing sound, a thick liquid gurgling, as he wrenched the weapon free. Her blood had begun to puddle on the worn carpet, and, as she still tried to crawl away, he could hear her breath rasping in the lung wound.

More of the crimson liquid was spilling over her lips and, when she finally clawed her way up onto the bed, he stood back for a second just watching her. She lay there, her chest rising and falling almost imperceptibly, the breath coming with difficulty, each inhalation bringing with it that vile sucking sound.

He moved towards the bed, the shaft of mirror still gripped firmly in his fist.

'You won't leave me,' he said, defiantly and the anger had returned to his voice. He grunted and drove the shard into her stomach, his own shouts now drowning her screams. The next thrust penetrated her heart and he recoiled as a powerful spout of blood exploded from the riven organ. Her body jerked spasmodically as he continued to plunge the razor sharp weapon into her, each thrust made her jump a little bit but the movements were also due to muscle spasm. Her fingers flexed and clenched then finally were still, her torn palm open.

By the time he had driven the glass into her for the twelfth time, her body no longer jerked and he fell, exhausted onto the bed beside her, the chunk of mirror still gripped firmly in his hand. He looked into her face, the eyes still open and staring at him in blank reproach, and, with his other hand, he gently touched her cheek. He wiped some blood away from the corners of her mouth, her swollen tongue lolling against his fingers as he did so.

Outside the room, Edward watched breathlessly, his eyes bulging. He watched as his father climbed onto the bed beside the bloodied rag which had once been Sheila. He saw the length of crystal clutched in his fist and he could hear him as he spoke.

'You can never leave me,' said Briggs, lying beside the body. His tone had softened now and he bent forward and kissed Sheila on the lips, ignoring the blood which he tasted. He lifted the piece of glass and held it against his throat, feeling its razor edge against his flesh. He pressed harder then, closing his eyes, he drew the piece of glass across the soft area just beneath his chin. The skin tore like rent fabric, blood vessels, severed by the passage of the weapon, spewed forth fountains of blood which seemed to hang in the air. Curving in crimson parabolas as they spurted from the ever widening cut. Like water from a broken dam the crimson fluid gushed out and Briggs rolled onto his back, his body quivering madly for long seconds, eyes rolling frenziedly in their sockets. He felt his bladder give out, the warm urine running down his leg and then, as blackness finally swept over him, his sphincter muscle failed.

They lay on the bed together, like discarded rag dolls.

Edward waited a few moments then opened the bedroom door. The stench which flooded over him was almost palpable and he recoiled momentarily, coughing as the pungent coppery odour of blood and the even more powerful stench of excrement assaulted his nostrils. He stood gazing at the two corpses on the bed, something in the back of his mind trying to convince him that these two blood-spattered objects had once been his parents. He was breathing slowly, sucking in breaths through his mouth to minimise the smell which filled the room. For long moments he stood motionless, gazing around the room which had been transformed into a charnel house then, slowly, he turned and made his way downstairs to the hall. There he dialled three nines and, when asked which service he required, called for both police and ambulance. He gave the address then slowly replaced the receiver before turning and making his way back up the stairs to the bedroom.

He had left the door open so now the smell had wafted out onto the landing too but Edward seemed not to notice it. He walked into the bedroom and sat down just inside the door, cross legged as if he were meditating, staring at the two bodies before him.

Maureen Briggs pushed open the front door and sighed, grateful to be home at last. The train from Victoria which she usually caught had been delayed because of some blockage in the tunnel so, instead of the tube, she had been forced to make the journey home by bus. Worse still, she noticed, one of the kids on the bus had smeared ice-cream on the back of her skirt. She muttered something to herself and wandered into the sitting room. The TV was still on but the room was empty, as was the kitchen, the dining room and the small extension which formed an extra part of the kitchen. In fact, except for the noise of the television, she noticed just how quiet the house was. It was going on for 6.50 p.m. there should be someone at home.

She headed back into the hall and began climbing the stairs, aware, as she reached half-way, of the smell which was coming from above her. She paused for a moment, brushing a strand of brown hair from her face, trying to figure out just what the hell was going on. She climbed the remaining steps and reached the landing where she spotted Edward sitting just inside the door to their parent's room.

She called his name and he looked round at her, his face blank and emotionless.

'I've called the police and the ambulance,' he said, quietly.

Her brow wrinkled and she moved towards the open door.

'What's wrong?' she asked.

'They're dead,' Edward told her, flatly.

She took a step into the room, her eyes widening as she scanned the carnage. For a second she swayed, not sure whether to scream or be sick but finally she found the breath for a scream.

Edward sat unmoved, gazing at the corpses, almost as if he didn't hear his sister.

In the distance he heard sirens and, slowly, he got to his feet.

Maureen had staggered from the room and was leaning against the bannister, her head spinning, stomach churning.

The noise of the sirens grew louder.

One

September 23rd, 1983:

The hammer drill hummed in Edward's grip as he held it, watching as the bit bored into the wall, spinning at over 2000 rpm. Small pieces of masonry fell to the ground, onto the newspaper which had been provided. He switched the drill off, blew some dust away from the hole and wiped the remainder away with his index finger.

'My husband's useless with tools,' said Michelle Peters, appearing at Edward's side. 'In fact he's only good for one thing when it comes to using his hands.' she giggled.

Edward coloured and did not turn to face her, in fact, as he reached for the first of the brackets he deliberately kept his head down so as to avoid her gaze. She was a young woman, yet to reach twenty-five and Edward cast her merely fleeting glances. She was dressed in a pair of red canvas dungarees and a yellow T-shirt and, from the way the material cut into her, Edward was convinced she wore nothing else. She padded around the house barefoot, chattering inanely to him as he worked, giggling every now and then at something she said. He watched her with contempt as she finally left the room, announcing that she was going to make a cup of tea.

He fitted the first bracket then set about preparing the second. The drill made a high-pitched screeching sound as it bit into the stonework and Edward was forced to stop once when a few minute pieces of brick flew back into his eye. He cursed and wiped them away with the corner of his handkerchief. He exhaled deeply and continued with the job.

There had been times during the past five years when he

had regretted taking over his father's business but there had been little choice for him. Maureen's wage was not enough to pay the rates and, besides, it was what his father would have wanted. Edward had managed to keep most of the regular customers as well as adding a few new ones too. Michelle Peters was one of the new ones. She padded back into the sitting room clutching two mugs of tea, one of which she set down near Edward who thanked her and carried on with his work.

'Are you married?' she asked him, sipping her tea.

'No,' he said, sharply.

'Girlfriend?'

He turned his back on her and pressed the button on the drill which sent it whirring into life again.

'I said have you got a girlfriend?' she asked, raising her voice above the scream of the drill.

He shook his head, wishing she would go away and leave him in peace. He felt uncomfortable in the company of women. He always had done and that feeling seemed to have been compounded since the death of his parents. He could sense them appraising him, especially the younger ones. Like this one. Some would try to flirt with him but Edward did not respond to their games. In truth he found them irritating. Why couldn't all women be like Maureen, he wondered? Even as he thought of her name a slight smile creased his face.

She had stayed with him during the past five years. They had lived together in the house, each needing the other. At least that was how it had been in the beginning. She had taken the death of their parents very badly. One of the many doctors he'd taken her to had told him that she had very nearly slipped into a catatonic state, such was the shock she had sustained. As it was she had spent two weeks in hospital recovering and it had taken all his powers of persuasion to talk her into staying on with him in the house. But then again, he reasoned, where would she have gone had she left? They had both led solitary lives and, as far as he knew, she had no friends with whom she could have stayed. So they had stopped on in the house. The door to his parents' room now firmly locked.

She had been in hospital when the funeral had taken place. There had been less than a dozen mourners, himself included and he remembered how it had rained that day and how the thin drizzle had covered everything like a film of gossamer. Even the flowers placed atop the coffins were coated with the moisture. They had been buried side by side. There had been a few people outside the gates of the cemetery. Journalists had come to the house shortly after the deaths had happened and they had questioned him even more exhaustively than the police. They had asked for permission to take pictures inside the house but Edward had refused.

He swallowed hard. Five years. It seemed like yesterday. The vision of what he had seen that day was burned indelibly into his memory and he doubted if it would ever be erased.

'Drink your tea before it gets cold.'

Michelle's voice, loud in his ear, sent the memories racing back to the recesses of his mind. There only to be mulled over in more private moments.

He switched off the drill and laid it down, reaching for his tea. There were pieces of dust floating on top and he removed them with his fingers, wiping them on his dark blue overalls.

Michelle was sitting on the sofa opposite him now, one leg drawn up beneath her, the mug of tea cradled in her lap.

Edward gave her a cursory glance as she swept her long black hair back.

'How come you haven't got a girlfriend?' she asked him.

Edward sighed.

'Does it really matter?' he said sharply.

'Just curious,' she said. 'Most blokes of your age are usually married. You're not even half-way there.' She chuckled.

He eyed her malevolently.

'I suppose you must meet a lot of women doing a job like

this,' she said. 'I mean, going into their houses and that. Haven't you ever tried it on with any of them? We had a bloke here not long ago to do the carpets, he was a real flirt. Quite dishy too. I nearly forgot I was married if you know what I mean?' She giggled again. A high pitched sound which grated on Edward's nerves. 'Haven't you ever fancied any of the women whose houses you've been in?'

He picked up the drill again, his fingers hovering over the button which would set the chuck spinning.

'Sometimes I feel like being a bit daring with the blokes who call here to do jobs,' she told him and giggled again. That grating giggle which so irritated him. 'You know, egging them on a bit, see if they fancy me and what they'll do about it.'

The drill roared into action, throbbing in Edward's grip. He held it firmly, staring at Michelle for long moments then he turned and, face flushed, drove the spinning bit into the wall. It penetrated the masonry, pushing deeper as he put his weight behind it. It continued to shriek and, for that he was thankful, at least he couldn't hear her giggling any longer. He gripped it until his knuckles turned white, pushing it further into the wall until the chuck itself struck stone. There was a thin film of perspiration covering his body and, when the drill was switched off, he could hear that familiar sound again.

He gritted his teeth.

When the hell was she going to stop giggling?

As Maureen Briggs opened the wooden gate which led up the short path to the front of the house she saw that the battered white Dolomite which Edward drove was parked in the gravel drive outside the garage. The office had closed at lunchtime for re-decorating and she had been able to get home relatively easily, avoiding the usual commuter débâcle which customarily accompanied her journeys to and from the office. She slowed her pace as she closed the gate behind her, sucking on the mint which she had in her mouth, hoping it would kill the smell of the drink.

Michael had taken her to the pub after they'd left work, persuading her that she had time for a drink before going home and, as usual, she had agreed with what he said.

She had been seeing Michael Ramsey for a little over six months now. They had worked in the same office for as long as she could remember and the relationship had simply grown. It had seemed a natural progression. From colleagues to friends and, finally, to lovers. Ramsey, like herself, had no parents but he had no family at all and that, Maureen thought was the thing which had brought them together, securing the bond even more.

Edward was ignorant of her involvement with Ramsey although she knew that sooner or later she would have to tell him. But, for now, she went through her little rituals of never mentioning his name (or the names of any other men come to that) and of doing things such as she was doing now. Sucking mints to disguise the smell of gin on her breath. She felt angry with herself for continuing with the self-imposed restraints which she had set, but it had seemed the best thing to do. She would rather lie to Edward than face endless hours of bickering and questioning. For the time being anyway.

That was one of the things she had noticed about him since the death of their parents. His attitude to her had become more than just protective. He had become possessive, jealous even. She only had to mention another man's name for him to fly into a rage – something else which annoyed her. She was growing tired of the house, her way of life and, if she was truthful, she was growing tired of Edward. She felt as if she were being smothered and now, as she approached the front door of the house, she shuddered involuntarily. It was as if it were sucking away at her soul, removing her hopes and desires. Replacing them instead with the knowledge that she was intended to live out the rest of her life in the place where she had grown up, sharing her dull existence with her older brother. She could see her own life mirrored in that of her late mother. The boredom, the sense of being trapped and now, in her case, of being shielded from the outside world.

She turned her key in the door and walked in.

Edward's tool bag was lying inside the hall, just where he always left it. Just where his father before him had left it. She took off her coat and hung it up, glancing at herself in the mirror, running a hand through her hair.

The house, as usual, was silent. She passed through the sitting room into the kitchen, muttering to herself. She decided to change before preparing the dinner.

Edward was at the top of the stairs, now dressed in a pair of trousers and a shirt, the collar button undone, the sleeves rolled up to reveal his thick forearms.

He seemed to appear from the shadows and Maureen stepped back in surprise.

'I didn't see you,' she said.

'I watched you come in,' he told her.

'Why didn't you say something?'

He shrugged.

'I'm going to get changed, then I'll start dinner,' she said.

Edward nodded. He paused for long moments looking at her and Maureen coloured. She felt naked before his gaze. He watched her as she disappeared inside her room then, slowly, he made his way down stairs again. A couple of the steps creaked and he made a mental note to fix them as soon as he got the time. Perhaps tonight.

It took Maureen just ten minutes to change and remove her make-up. That done, she went back to the kitchen wearing a thin sweater and a pair of jeans, one back pocket of which had been used to patch a threaded knee. She found Edward sitting at the table looking abstractedly at the evening paper which had just arrived.

'You could have laid the table,' she said, exasperatedly.

'I never thought,' he said.

23

'Well try thinking, Edward, please. I go out to work too you know. If we're living here together we ought to share the chores.'

He smiled thinly.

'Living together,' he said. 'You make it sound as if we're lovers.'

Maureen did not look at him, she merely crossed to the freezer and took out a couple of packets of frozen vegetables, tipping measured amounts into two saucepans which stood on the cooker.

'You should try to help around the house,' she said. 'I mean if I should leave or – '

He cut her short.

'Leave? What do you mean leave?' There was a harshness to his voice, a probing vehemence which made her realize just how hard it was going to be when she eventually *did* have to tell him about Ramsey.

'Or if something happened to me,' she added hastily. 'What would you do then?'

'I'd manage,' he told her. 'I'm not helpless.'

'So why don't you do something to help me now?' she said, adjusting the flame beneath one of the saucepans.

'Like what?' he asked.

'Lay the table,' she said, irritably. 'Christ, Edward, sometimes you act as if . . .' She let the sentence trail off.

'As if we're married?' he said and she wasn't sure whether it came out as a question or a statement. He smiled again and crossed to one of the drawers, taking out a tablecloth and a handful of cutlery. She watched him for a moment wondering just when would be the right moment to tell him of her plans. She shook her head. Plans? She didn't even have any plans. She wanted to get out of the house, away from Edward and this suffocating life-style, that much she knew. She also knew that she loved Michael Ramsey, wanted to be with him. Perhaps that was her way out. Ramsey had his own flat in Finsbury. She'd been there with him on a number of occasions, sometimes for hurried lunch-time lovemaking. She knew he would be delighted if

24

she moved in with him. The thought was an attractive one. But, as she watched Edward laying the table she felt those irritatingly conflicting emotions rising within her again. She longed to be away from the house, from Edward, but she also pitied him. There was no love there, none of the usual brother/sister affection. She was with him because she felt she owed it to him. He had, after all, been immensely supportive after the death of their parents. That much she owed him but, she reasoned, should she let that debt ruin the rest of her life?

She pushed the steak and kidney pie into the oven and checked her watch.

'Why are you home so early?' he asked her, sitting down once more.

She told him about the re-decorating.

'Did you see anyone on the way home?' he wanted to know.

She looked at him suspiciously.

'Like who?'

He shrugged.

'Friends. People from your office.'

She opened her mouth to speak but then changed her mind. It wasn't the time to mention Ramsey. Not yet.

'I went for a drink with one of the girls before I came home,' she told him.

He looked at her, impassively.

'What did you talk about?' he wanted to know.

'The things women talk about. Things that don't interest men.' She smiled, humourlessly. Then, anxious to change the subject:

'What have you been doing?'

He told her about Michelle Peters.

'Why are women like that?' he said, almost angrily, as if Maureen could supply him with the answer. 'They flirt, they try to make fools out of men.'

She frowned.

'Not all women are like that, Edward,' she said.

He looked at her, allowing his eyes to linger just a fraction too long on her breasts which she covered with her arms, crossing them before her, once more feeling naked as he looked at her.

'I know,' he said. 'Not all of them.'

The aroma of cooking food began to fill the kitchen and Maureen reached up to the knife rack which had been secured in place above one of the draining boards. Twelve knives of varying sizes hung from it, along with a perforated spoon and a large cleaver. She selected a knife and prodded the vegetables.

Even with her back to him, she could feel his eyes boring into her and, indeed, he watched her as she attended to the food allowing his gaze to travel down from her lustrous brown hair to her slender shoulders, pausing briefly to follow the outline of her bra beneath the sweater and then down to trace the smooth curve of her buttocks. He could feel a warmth beginning to grow around his groin and the first stirrings of an erection began to form a bulge in his trousers.

Without turning to face him, Maureen said:

'This won't be ready for a few minutes. I'll call you when it's on the table.'

He nodded, although she couldn't see him. For long seconds he lingered then she heard the scraping of wood on vinyl as he pushed his chair back and left the kitchen. She breathed an audible sigh which was something akin to relief.

The water in the pans bubbled furiously.

Two

Neither of them said much as they sat at opposite ends of the table eating. One of the fluorescent lights in the central bank kept flickering and Edward made a mental note to fix that as well as the creaking steps. It was raining lightly outside and, but for the gentle tapping of the rain on the large windows and the persistent hum of the fluorescents, the kitchen was silent. The blinds had been dropped, shutting out the night sky which was mottled blue and black. Traffic in the street outside passed by soundlessly, any noise muffled by the soundproofing which surrounded the large dwelling in a glove of perpetual solitude. The absence of outside noise made those sounds inside seem all the more noticeable and, more than once, Maureen looked up at the buzzing lights which hummed like indolent flies.

They washed up and retreated into the sitting room.

She tried to read while Edward watched television. There was a comedy programme on but he watched it impassively, not so much as grinning even when the studio audience went into paroxysms of 'canned' mirth.

Maureen put the book down and massaged the bridge of her nose between thumb and forefinger. She glanced at her watch and then at the large antique clock on the mantelpiece above the fire. Its ponderous ticking seemed even louder than usual.

It was 10.15 p.m.

'I'm going to have a bath and then I'm going to bed,' said Maureen. 'Is there anything you want before I go?'

He looked at her then shook his head.

They exchanged brief 'goodnights' and she left the room, pleased to be out of the oppressive atmosphere. As she climbed the stairs she wondered just how much more of it she could take.

Edward listened to her footsteps on the staircase, able to tell exactly where she was by the creaks which accompanied her ascent. He continued to gaze blankly at the screen before him, his eyes glazed. Then, he got to his feet and switched the set off. The silence descended like an invisible shroud, broken only by the ever-present ticking of the clock. But, as he sat motionless in the chair, Edward heard the sounds of water running, the loud splashes as Maureen spun both taps to fill the bath. He looked at the clock, watching as the minute hand marked off five intervals, then he heard the noise from upstairs stop. He got to his feet and walked slowly out into the short corridor which led to the hall. Maureen had not bothered to turn on any lights and Edward was quite content to move around in the darkness. He paused at the bottom of the stairs, gazing up into the gloom in the direction of the bathroom. As quickly and quietly as he could, he scuttled up to the landing.

He paused briefly at the bathroom door then he hurried into his bedroom and closed the door behind him. He moved in the blackness with ease, as if the light offended him, finally coming to a photograph which hung next to his wardrobe. It was a large, framed effort of his parents, taken many years ago and now cracked in places. He hurriedly removed it and laid it on the bed.

He had made the peephole some five years ago, shortly before the death of his parents and it gave him a clear view of the bathroom and anyone inside. Carefully masked on the other side to prevent discovery, it was like a tiny window to him and now, excitedly, he pressed his eye to it.

Maureen had her back to him, studying her reflection in the mirror on the far wall. She ran a hand through her hair pausing momentarily to look at the dark rings which had formed beneath her eyes. She sighed and began to undress.

Edward watched, mesmerised, as she pulled her sweater off, kicking her slippers alongside it. She popped open the button of her jeans and unzipped them and he watched delightedly as she pulled them off. Already he could feel his erection beginning to strain against his trousers and, as Maureen reached round to unhook her bra, his breathing became more rapid. Loud. He tried to control it, afraid that she might hear him, but she did not and he ran his gaze over her taut breasts, lingering on the nipples for tantalising moments before allowing his eyes to shift their centre of interest. She removed her panties and tossed them aside, standing naked for a second before climbing into the bath. He whimpered softly and rubbed his stiffness through his trousers. He could hear her splashing about in the bath, watched as she soaped herself, hands slipping over her body as they glided on the creamy foam. He watched the water glistening on her breasts, running between their valley. And he saw the dark triangle of her pubic hair beneath the surface.

He watched her until she clambered out of the bath and began to dry herself then he reached for the photograph and, carefully, replaced it over the peephole. He sat on the edge of his bed, listening to the sound of the water as it sucked down the plughole, the only sound in the deathly silence which filled the house like some living thing, pushing the walls outward as it seemed to grow in intensity. Edward listened to the sound of his own breathing, harsh but a little slower now and he felt his erection still strong within the confines of his trousers. He lay back on the bed, gazing at the ceiling. There were no cracks, just the smooth surface which his father had applied, what seemed like an eternity ago. Visions floated through his mind. His father. His mother. The slaughter that he had witnessed in the locked room just up the hall.

And Maureen.

He felt his penis throb with renewed vigour and he whispered her name softly.

Edward moved silently through the darkened house, the key ring in the pocket of his dressing gown. He enjoyed the darkness and solitude which the dwelling offered and it reminded him of a church so hushed and still was it. He moved about without turning on lights and, when he reached the cellar door, he already had his hand on the appropriate key. He turned it in the lock and pushed the door open, reaching for the light switches just inside.

The fluorescents spluttered for a second then burst into life, bathing the cellar in cold white light. Edward closed the door behind him and wandered down the narrow steps.

The subterranean part of the house was colder, having no form of heating except the paraffin stove which stood neglected in one corner. The cellar itself was large. Painted white and tiled, it was fully forty feet long and about half that in width. There was a large work bench in the centre of the room, equipped with a vice. There were a couple of chisels and a claw hammer lying close by and Edward picked up the heavy object, hefting it before him, touching the two thick prongs with his thumb. He replaced it and moved across to the saw bench, lifting the protective cover to expose the vicious circular blade beneath. The teeth on the blade were like hooks and Edward touched them almost lovingly. There was a dark stain on the wood, one which had been there for as long as he could remember. His father had bought it from another carpenter many years ago and Edward remembered his father telling him how the stain got there. The man had been using the saw bench to cut a particularly large piece of timber. He had slipped, the wood spinning from his grasp as the blade hit a knot-hole and the vicious circular blade, its motor turning it at over 1500 rpm, had sliced through his palm just above the wrist, ripping the flesh open and churning the bone to pulp as it tore his arm to ribbons as far as the elbow. The elbow itself had been splintered into a hundred fragments and, the damage done to the limb had been so great that the only solution had been amputation.

Edward looked at the dark blood stain, now a feature of the saw-bench and gently lowered the protective cover back into place.

There were metal cabinets full of screw-drivers, chisels, drill bits, pliers and countless other tools. All of them were carefully marked with a sticky label according to their weight and usage and each one was kept oiled and clean. His father had been a methodical man and Edward had followed his example. Screws, rivets and nails were similarly marked, according to thread and size.

The power tools were in a cabinet on their own, beside the endless lengths of timber and, as Edward wandered the cellar, the smell of wood was strong in his nostrils. He paused for a moment, his hand on a power drill and, all at once, thoughts began to flood into his mind. Strange unwelcome thoughts. Fears even.

Maureen had mentioned leaving. Mentioned it only in passing admittedly but she had not spoken of it before. Why now, he wondered? She had been angry, he told himself, she had asked him how he would manage *if* she left, not *when* she left. He held the drill before him. Was this, he wondered, how his father had felt when he learned that Sheila was leaving him? Edward put the drill down. No. Maureen had not said she intended leaving.

He stood in the silence for a second and yet, could he expect her to stay with him forever? There would be men who wanted her. She was a very attractive girl, it was only natural that other men should desire her.

As he himself did.

He swallowed hard.

What if she was already seeing another man? Like his mother had done. Deceiving his father all that time.

No, Maureen was different.

He opened another cabinet, a larger one and lifted the chainsaw out, laying it on the work bench. It was heavy, fifteen pounds, but Edward hardly noticed its bulk as he held it before him, studying the sixteen inch blade, the vicious hooks set in every other link of the chain which ran around the polished metal. It was a McCullough, a powerful tool, able to cut through wood as thick as forty inches at a stroke. He had even seen it plough through metal. He didn't have much use for it but, just like all the other equipment and tools he owned, he kept it oiled and in perfect working order. He lifted it once more, running a hand over the savage, barbed, chain, careful not to cut himself on the teeth.

Did Maureen love him as much as *he* loved her?

He doubted it for his love had turned to lust. Affection had been transformed into desire and protectiveness had become obsessive jealousy.

The doors of the cellar bulkhead rattled as a particularly strong gust of wind swept over them.

Edward looked at the chainsaw once more then slowly and carefully replaced it in the cupboard.

He wandered back up the stairs, flicked off the lights and locked the cellar door behind him. He twisted the handle to make sure it was secure then he dropped the keys into his pocket and moved quietly back upstairs. The steps creaked beneath his weight as he climbed upward but he didn't worry about the noise. He knew it would not wake Maureen. She had taken sleeping pills for the last five years, ever since the death of their parents. At first she had been plagued by terrible nightmares and the pills had been effective in staving off those monstrous visions. She continued taking them out of habit as much as anything else.

Indeed, as Edward opened the door of her bedroom and stepped in, she did not even stir.

He pushed the door to but did not close it. He moved slowly around the bed, noticing the bottle of Mogadon on her sideboard as he did so. Her clothes were draped over a chair in one corner of the room and Edward crossed to them, reaching for her tiny panties. He held them before him for a second, the familiar warmth in his groin beginning to spread, then he pressed them to his face, kissing the gusset clumsily. His erection grew stronger and, replacing the panties, he moved closer to the bed and looked down at Maureen. She was lying on her back, hair smeared across her face, sheets and covers pulled up to cover her neck.

Edward's hands trembled slightly as he reached for the

covers and pulled them back. She moaned slightly in her sleep and he froze, but her breathing settled once again into a more rhymthic pattern and he continued pulling the covers.

Maureen was wearing a short nightie. In the darkness he couldn't be sure of the colour but, he could see the dark outline of her nipples and pubic hair through the thin material. Her left leg was drawn up slightly and he ran his eyes over its firm slimness wanting so badly to touch her but not daring to. He moved closer to the bed and, with infinite care, took hold of the bottom of the nightie. Holding his breath, he raised it until it was almost around her neck, her breasts and mound now fully visible to him. He watched the gentle rise and fall of her chest, his eyes straying to her nipples then down to her pubic bush, her legs slightly parted.

For long moments he gazed at her then, closing the door behind him, he padded back to his own bedroom.

He lay in the darkness, gazing at his own ceiling, a slight smile creasing his face.

No. Maureen would not leave him.

Three

Maureen smiled as she saw Michael Ramsey trying to weave his way through the bustle of people, carrying the tray as if it were stacked with hand grenades instead of two plough-man's lunches. The drinks wobbled precariously as Ramsey made his way back to the table and, more than once, he had to perform what amounted to a juggling act to prevent the entire tray tipping up. But, he finally made it and set the lunches down on the table.

'It's like going through a minefield on a pogo stick trying to carry anything in here,' said Ramsey, sitting down beside her.

She smiled and squeezed his hand.

The pub was even busier than usual, it seemed, and people swarmed around the bar like flies round a dead dog. In one corner of the room a group of youths were leaning on the juke-box which was thundering out a tune that almost shook the tables nearby. Smoke from countless cigarettes drifted in the air like some kind of man-made fog and Ramsey waved a hand in front of his face in an effort to disperse some of it. Maureen, her mouth full of cheese and pickle, watched him.

He was dressed in a navy blue suit, slightly shiny on the elbows but, nevertheless immaculately clean and pressed. His face was strong but lacked any harshness of features. Black hair curled to just above the collar of his shirt and, when he drank, the froth from his beer stuck to his moustache. Maureen wiped it off, chuckling. He thanked her and, when he spoke, she could hear just how strong his accent was.

Ramsey had been born in Derbyshire. His mother had died in child-birth and his father, a miner, had been killed in a pit accident. He had spent the rest of his teenage years in a succession of foster homes, finally moving to London when he was nineteen. Now, twelve years later, he had a flat of his own and a steady job. And, with Maureen, he had something else too. He had love. They had been attracted to each other from the beginning, he himself feeling that their relationship was stronger because of their backgrounds, in as much as both were without parents. She had told him the truth of how her mother and father had died, feeling ashamed as she did so but, nonetheless thinking that he *should* know. And, afterwards, she had wept. He had never met the brother she spoke of, at times guardedly, but from what little he did know, he realized just what she had to put up with. More than once he had considered asking her to move away from Edward, to come and live in his flat instead. But, each time, he had lost his nerve. He loved her and he knew she loved him but, somewhere at the back of his mind, there was the ever-present fear of refusal. Now he watched her as she ate, pushing small pieces of food into her mouth, chewing indifferently.

'Something on your mind?' he asked.

She smiled and shook her head.

'You're not a very good liar, Maureen,' he said, raising his eyebrows quizzically.

She exhaled deeply.

'It's Edward,' she told him and Ramsey was surprised that she mentioned her brother's name so readily.

'What about him?' he wanted to know.

'I don't know what it is, Mike.' She sipped her drink. 'He's becoming more and more . . .' She struggled to find the word.

'Difficult?' he offered.

She related their conversation of the previous night and Ramsey listened with interest, noting how tired she looked, as if even talking about it were an effort. He allowed her to finish then took a long swallow of his beer before speaking.

'Well, he's going to have to get used to the idea of you leaving one day,' he said.

'But that's the whole point,' she told him. 'I hardly mentioned it. I didn't even say anything about leaving him and he started to get angry. Angry or frightened, I'm not sure which.'

'So what are you going to do? Let him ruin your life for you? He's got no right to expect you to stay with him, to live the way he lives.'

'That's easy for you to say, Mike but I can't just pack up and move out.'

'Why not? Edward's not a child anymore. He can look after himself. He'll have to *learn* to look after himself.'

There was a long silence between them, finally broken by Ramsey.

'Can you come to my place tonight?' he asked her. 'We can talk about it.' He smiled and she gripped his hand tightly.

She nodded.

'About eight?'

'Yes,' she said.

He nodded towards the plate of food.

'Eat your lunch,' he said, smiling.

Maureen glanced at her watch and then at the electric clock on the wall of the kitchen. The hands had crawled round to 6.56 p.m. She looked across the table at Edward who had finished his dinner and was looking at her and she had the ridiculous feeling that he could somehow read her mind. He *knew* what she was thinking. She smiled as brightly as she was able and got to her feet.

'I'm going to leave you to wash up, Edward,' she said. 'I'm going to get ready.'

He fixed his gaze on her.

'Ready for what?' he asked, a hard edge to his voice.

'I'm going out,' she told him and made for the door.

36

He shot out a hand and gripped her wrist and she almost gasped aloud at the strength in that grip.

'Where are you going?' he wanted to know.

She swallowed hard.

'Let go of my arm, Edward.'

'I asked where you were going.'

She pulled away, angrily.

'I'm going out,' she rasped. 'It's not really any of your business where I'm going.'

'You're meeting a man aren't you?' he said and she felt herself colour like some disobedient child whose secret has just been discovered.

'Would it make any difference if I was?' she asked, knowing full well what his answer would be.

'Is it a man?' he snarled, getting to his feet and, for brief seconds, she thought he was going to strike her.

'Yes.'

He swallowed hard.

'Who is he?' Edward demanded.

'His name is Michael Ramsey, I've been seeing him for over six months now.'

That was it said, she thought. It had come out almost as a confession but, at least she had finally told him. They faced each other in silence for long moments and she found that her breath was coming in short gasps. Edward didn't speak. His eyes were bulging wide, his body quivering almost imperceptibly and he looked as though he was in pain but then, almost contemptuously, he turned his back on her and began clearing the table, dropping the plates and cutlery into the sink with a succession of loud crashes. She watched him for a moment then retreated from the kitchen. Edward heard her footsteps on the stairs as she ascended. He gritted his teeth and held onto the edge of the sink.

Another man.

He had wondered how long it would be before this happened. Would this man be the first? Had he been the latest in a long list of men she had met secretly behind his back? He watched the water gushing into the sink and felt

37

the anger rising within him. He plunged his hands into the sink, barely noticing how hot the water was. As he removed each plate he jammed it into the drainer, the last one knocking the knife rack to his left.

The row of blades jangled noisily, the cold white light of the fluorescents reflecting off their glinting edges.

Maureen stayed in her room until the taxi pulled up in front of the house. She knew that if she spoke to Edward again, there would inevitably be arguments and she did not want that. She smoothed out a crease in her grey skirt and made her way hurriedly down the stairs to the front door. As she opened it she paused, looking in the direction of the sitting room. The door was ajar and the television was on.

'I won't be late, Edward,' she called but received no answer.

She pulled the door shut behind her and scuttled out to the waiting taxi.

Up in his bedroom, Edward watched her as she climbed into the waiting cab. In the faint glow of the street lamp he studied her shadowy form, teeth gritted, the knot of muscles at the side of his jaw pulsing angrily.

The taxi drove off.

Four

Maureen held the brandy glass in her hand and gazed into the dark fluid, inhaling the strong aroma of the liquor. She sipped it, feeling the alcohol burn its way to her stomach to join the Beef Stroganoff which she and Ramsey had eaten just an hour before. He had cooked it himself, the tempting aroma had greeted her at the door of the flat as he'd opened it and now she sat back on his couch feeling pleasantly full. The record player was on, a tune she recognised but could not put a name to. It seemed to drift through the air like the smoke from his cigar. Maureen pressed herself closer to Ramsey and laid her head on his shoulder.

'I've missed too much during my life,' she said, wistfully. 'There haven't been too many nights like this.'

'I know what you mean,' Ramsey echoed, sliding one arm around her shoulder.

She glanced around the room. It was tastefully decorated, the cream-coloured walls adorned here and there with paintings. The simple water colours were Ramsey's own work but they were a window to the man's sensitivity which Maureen found beguiling. It was one of the many facets of his character which made him so attractive to her. To look at his large hands, anyone not familiar with him would have thought them more likely to be used for a rough manual job and not the relaxing pasttime of art. But he was skilled in his hobby and he took pride in the works hanging on the walls.

The place was spotlessly clean, like Ramsey himself and, as Maureen moved closer to him, she detected the odour of after-shave.

She hiccuped and rubbed her stomach apologetically.

They both laughed and then, slowly, she turned her head and kissed him. His response was intense, each of them seeking the warm moistness of the other's tongue and, when they finally parted, he stroked her cheek gently.

'Edward knows,' she said, quietly.

'About us?' said Ramsey.

She nodded.

'What did he say?'

'Not much. He didn't have to say anything, if you know what I mean'

He did.

'So what do you do now?' he asked.

'I don't know,' she said. 'But I'm glad he knows, even though it might have hurt him. I couldn't have gone on much longer trying to hide it from him. I feel better now it's out in the open.'

'You make it sound as if you've committed a crime,' he said.

She laughed humourlessly.

'You should have seen the way he looked at me when I told him about you and I.' She shuddered involuntarily. There was a long pause. 'I don't think I can carry on living in that house, Mike. I don't think I want to.'

He swallowed hard.

'So move out,' he said, nervously. 'This flat is too big for one anyway.'

She looked at him, a slight smile on her lips.

'Move in with you?' It came out more as a statement than a question.

He nodded. Was she going to refuse him? He wondered if he had asked too early.

'I don't know how Edward would take it,' she said, softly.

'Yes you do,' Ramsey said, wearily. He'll moan and groan, he might even shout a bit. Whatever the case he won't want you to leave. The point is, do you want to leave?'

'Of course I do,' she said. 'I've just told you, but it's not that easy.'

'Why?' he demanded. 'You want to get out, I'm offering you somewhere . . .' He hesitated. 'Somewhere permanent.'

She looked at him again.

'I love you, Maureen,' he said. 'I want you with me and if that sounds like a proposal then . . . OK'

She touched his lips with her finger.

'When could I move in?' she asked, smiling.

They both put their drinks down and moved closer, Maureen snaking her hands up around his neck, pulling his mouth against hers. Without breaking the kiss, he pulled her legs around until her knees were across his thighs then, he slid one powerful arm beneath her legs and the other around her back and, effortlessly, lifted her up. She giggled as he carried her towards the bedroom, finally laying her gently on top of the quilt. She raised one knee and her skirt slipped down exposing one smooth thigh. Ramsey climbed onto the bed beside her, his hands working swiftly but tenderly, one undoing the buttons of her blouse, the other gently stroking her hair.

She herself reached for the zip of his trousers, feeling the growing bulge beneath. She whispered his name softly as he unhooked her bra and pulled it free, exposing her breasts. He kissed each in turn, feeling the nipples harden beneath the attention of his tongue and she gasped as his tongue flicked lower, her own hands now releasing the clasp of her skirt. She raised her buttocks and pulled the garment free, lying back to watch as he pulled off his shirt and trousers. She traced the outline of his muscles with her eyes, his thick arms engulfing her as he re-joined her on the bed, pulling at her panties, eager to reach the silky moistness beyond. Once more she lifted herself up to allow him freedom to remove the piece of clothing and, finally, they lay naked together, each feeling the heat of the other's body.

Her hand gripped his swollen penis, pulling him onto

her. For long moments she felt the head of his shaft nudging her vagina and then, with a movement which took her breath away, he thrust into her. They both gasped as the movements began. Slow, rhythmic strokes which seemed to send waves of pleasure the entire length of her body and she raised her knees to allow him deeper penetration. He began to move faster inside her and she gripped his shoulders, raking the flesh with her nails as she felt her climax building.

He sensed her growing excitement and speeded up, his own orgasm now approaching. She bucked wildly beneath him and the increased pressure on his penis as her muscles tightened brought him to the peak with her. Both of them gasped aloud, the cries diminishing as he slowed his movements until they finally lay still in each other's arms. He kissed her forehead and then her lips, holding her close to him for long seconds before rolling off. She moved onto her side, fingers tracing patterns in the hair on his chest, gliding down to his navel and then beyond to stroke his, now flaccid, penis.

'I love you,' she whispered.

He reached down and pulled the quilt over them. They lay in the darkness of the room, not bothering to switch on the bedside lamp, satisfied with the dim glow of the sodium street light which filtered in from outside.

'When will you tell Edward that you're leaving?' he asked.

She sighed.

'Oh God,' she murmured. 'I'd almost forgotten about that.'

'Changed your mind about moving in with me?'

She wriggled closer to him.

'No,' she said. 'Of course I haven't but, as I said, it isn't going to be easy telling him.'

'Would you like me to come with you? If I met him . . .'

Maureen cut him short.

'No,' she said. 'I must tell him myself. Try to make him understand.' She was silent for a long time.

'You musn't pity him, Maureen,' said Ramsey. 'You can't let him ruin your life. He'll come to terms with it in time. Just think about yourself for once. Do what's right for *you*.'

She nodded and kissed him on the cheek.

'What time is it?' she wanted to know.

He glanced at his watch.

'Nearly eleven.'

She swung herself out of bed and began retrieving her clothes.

'I'd better leave, can you call me a taxi, please?'

He nodded, pulled his trousers on and padded into the sitting room. She heard the numbers on the dial clicking round and then his voice.

When she was dressed she walked back into the other room.

'It'll be here in five minutes,' he told her.

She pulled on her coat.

'Would you like another drink before you go?' he asked.

She raised one eyebrow.

'Dutch courage?' she said.

'Is it really as bad as that?'

She smiled thinly.

'He'll be all right, once I've explained everything to him.'

Will he? she asked herself. Is it going to be that easy? She shuddered again. No, it wasn't going to be that easy.

There was a strident blast as the taxi sounded its hooter and Ramsey peered out of the window, waving at the driver to acknowledge his presence. He returned to Maureen and took her in his arms, kissing her. They finally parted and he stroked her cheek.

'Call me if you need any help,' he said. 'Like I said if I talk to him . . .'

Again she cut him short.

'I'll be OK, Mike,' she reassured him and headed for the door.

They kissed once more then she was gone.

Ramsey closed the door behind her and slid the bolt across. Outside, he heard the taxi revving up and, when he crossed to the window and looked out, it was gone.

The cab driver asked Maureen where she wanted to go and then proceeded to regale her with details of the difficult customer he'd just dropped off. She heard the words but none of them made sense for her mind was elsewhere. She gazed out of the side window but saw only her own reflection in the blackness. Perhaps Edward would be in bed when she got home. If she could tell him in the morning, he might have cooled off by then. Perhaps, in the cold light of day, he would see reason.

The taxi braked sharply to avoid a speeding car which cut across in front of it and Maureen looked up startled.

'Stupid bastard,' the driver yelled after the speeding vehicle. 'I reckon some of these silly fuckers take their tests at St. Dunstan's,' he said, irritably, driving on.

Maureen slumped back in the seat again, eyes closed. The journey from Ramsey's flat to their own house usually took about twenty-five minutes but, with less traffic on the road, the driver made good time and, as she opened her eyes, she saw that he was approaching the house. Framed by scudding banks of rain clouds it looked strangely menacing and, for fleeting seconds, Maureen had the ridiculous notion of telling the man to keep driving. To get her away from this gaunt edifice which stifled her as surely as a pillow across her face.

She pointed out the building, paid the driver and made her way up the short path to the front door. There wasn't a single light on in the house and, as she twisted her key in the front door, the blackness seemed to envelop her. As if it were flowing from inside the dwelling itself. She closed the door and the darkness was joined by the customary silence. Both seemed to close around her and she slapped at the light switch, breathing more easily when the hall lit up. She hung

44

up her coat, noticing that Edward's tool bag was still lying where he had left it.

She pushed open the door of the sitting room and walked in.

It too was in darkness, only the meagre light from the hall filtering in to break the totality of the gloom. The silence seemed to thicken. She realized that Edward must be upstairs.

'You said you'd be early.'

She almost shouted aloud in surprise when she heard his voice. It came to her through the darkness and she felt her heart thud hard against her ribs.

'You frightened me,' she said. 'Why are you sitting in the dark?' She crossed to the lamp on the TV and flicked it on. A puddle of light formed beneath it.

'Why didn't you put the light on?' she asked him.

'I've been thinking,' he said.

'About what?'

She knew very well.

'About you and this man,' he said scornfully.

'We have to talk about it, Edward. We have to talk about it sensibly.'

'Is that where you've been until now?' he rasped. 'With this man?'

She was annoyed by the tone of his voice.

'Yes I have. There's nothing wrong with that.'

'You should have told me about him before.'

'Why should I tell you everything that I do? It's my life, I'll live it the way I want to.'

'Is he the first?'

She looked puzzled.

'What do you mean?' she asked him.

'Is he the first man you've been to bed with?'

'That's none of your business, Edward.' She was finding it difficult to keep her temper.

He got to his feet.

'It *is* my business,' he insisted.

She turned and walked into the kitchen, aware that he

45

was close behind her. She flicked on the lights and the fluorescents sputtered into life. She crossed to the sink and filled the kettle.

'I love him, Edward,' she said, facing her brother.

His face dropped, the colour draining from it.

'I'm going to live with him,' she added.

'Live with him?' he repeated. 'You mean you're going to leave me?'

'Yes,' she said, softly, hesitantly.

He looked hurt and she felt that familiar feeling of pity rising once again but she fought it back, determined not to weaken.

'Why are you leaving me? he asked, mournfully.

'I've told you, I'm going to live with Mike. I love him.'

'But I love *you*,' he rasped, fists bunching at his sides.

'Edward, I'm not happy here,' she said, her breath coming in gasps. This isn't the way I want to live the rest of my life. With Mike I've got something. I need him.'

'Yes, you need him to fuck you,' he snarled. 'Did he fuck you tonight?'

'Don't you speak to me like that,' she said.

'DID HE?'

She felt her hands trembling slightly.

'I think it best if I left now,' she said.

His tone changed abruptly, the note of pleading, of hurt had returned to it.

'I don't want you to leave, Maureen,' he said.

'For God's sake, Edward, can't you see what these past five years have done to me? This isn't a house anymore, it's a prison and you've been acting like a warder. I can't take it anymore. I've found a man I love and who loves me. I'm leaving.'

'You're just like mother was,' he bellowed, the anger now back in his voice. 'She was a whore. She betrayed father. She was fucked by another man and she was going to leave but he stopped her.'

Maureen felt suddenly afraid. She took a step backwards, seeing how close she was to the kitchen door should she

46

have to make a dash for it. But, he saw her eyes dart in that direction and he moved across towards the door.

'Edward,' she said. 'I wanted to talk about this rationally, without either of us getting worked up.'

'No,' he hissed through clenched teeth. 'You wanted to leave me. Leave *our* house, just like mother did. I heard them that day you know. She was going to leave father for another man, she told him so. I thought *you* were different. The women that I meet when I'm working, most of them are sluts but I always thought that you were different. But you're not. You're a filthy little slut too,' He sucked in a deep breath. 'I won't let you leave me, Maureen.' He stepped forward and grabbed her arm but she shook loose, finding a strength born of fear. He stumbled backwards, his hand trailing along the draining board. Plates and cups were sent crashing to the ground.

She moved for the door.

'No,' he roared, his hand closing around the wooden handle of the cleaver which hung alongside the numerous blades on the rack.

She tugged at the door but he had locked it and he stood between her and the door to the sitting room.

The heavy blade of the cleaver sparkled as he hefted it before him.

'Edward, for God's sake,' she whimpered. 'All right, I'll call Mike, tell him I'm staying here.'

He shook his head, a crooked grin creasing his face.

'You won't trick me like that,' he said. He lowered the cleaver slightly. '*I* love you, Maureen, why do you need *him*?'

'Edward, please put the cleaver down,' she said.

'We belong together,' he whispered, raising the blade once more. His eyes were bulging madly, the whites crisscrossed by tendrils of red vein.

'You won't leave me alone,' he said and swung at her.

The kettle began to boil , its high pitched squeal mingling with Maureen's own shriek of terror as the cleaver swept down towards her. The wicked blade buried itself in the table top but Edward wrenched it free, knocking the table aside in his efforts to reach his sister.

She picked up a chair and held it before her but, with three powerful blows, he reduced it to matchwood.

'You are mine, Maureen,' he proclaimed, standing less than a foot from her.

The kettle continued to shriek.

Edward brought the cleaver down with as much power as he could muster, the muscles in his arms bulging. The blade caught Maureen at the point of neck and shoulder, smashing her clavical and exposing a mess of torn muscle and tendon. Severed arteries spewed forth streamers of blood which spattered Edward. He grabbed his sister by the hair and threw her across the room where she slammed into the draining board.

Moaning softly, aware of the gouts of blood spurting from her neck, she managed to tug the largest of the kitchen knives from its position on the rack and, as Edward advanced on her, she struck out blindly with it.

The point of the blade caught the end of his nose and gouged out a sizeable lump of flesh. He shrieked as his own blood began to spill onto the lino, mingling with that of his sister.

He struck again, his second blow severing the hand which held the knife. The hand, still clutching the blade, spun into the air and landed in the sink.

Maureen dropped to her knees, the stump of her arm held before her. Her clothes were drenched in blood, the coppery stench filling her nostrils and, as well as the blood, she noticed the puddle of urine between her legs. The thick crimson fluid filled her mouth and, when she coughed, purple foam oozed over her lips. She raised her head, seeing that Edward was upon her, realizing that this was the end.

She thought of Ramsey.

Edward swung the cleaver a third time, shouting something as he did so. It sliced through Maureen's neck and he heard a sharp crack as several bones in her spinal cord were splintered under the impact. A fresh eruption of blood accompanied the blow and her head sagged first to one side and then forward. She toppled across a chair, head down, blood splashing noisily onto the lino. Her hair hung in matted strands, uncovering the back of her neck and, with one final maniacal swipe, Edward brought the cleaver down again.

This time the splintering of bone was louder as the wicked blade sheared through her neck just above the shoulder. The head came free, propelled several feet across the floor by the impact of the strike. It rolled over and over until it finally came to rest on the stump, eyes open and staring accusingly. Edward crossed to it and picked it up by the hair, gazing into the eyes. His body ached and his nose was throbbing where Maureen had cut it but he seemed unconcerned, his gaze fixed on the severed head which he held. Strands of torn flesh and tiny pieces of bone hung from what was left of the neck, the blood which had been gushing from the hewn appendage now reduced to little more than a trickle.

He put the head down on the table and crossed to the sink, looking in at the hand. Her hand. The knife still gripped in rigored fingers. He lifted it out, tugging the blade free with difficulty. He hurriedly washed his own hands in the sink, aware too that the kettle was still boiling. He reached over and turned it off, the usual silence descending rapidly to envelop him once more. He stood breathless for long seconds, pressing against the cupboards which were below the sink and, for the first time, he noticed that he had a strong erection. He looked at the blood spattered body of Maureen and found that the throbbing between his legs was even more powerful but he tried to force the thoughts to the back of his mind. He had other things to do.

Standing in the middle of the kitchen he stripped naked, piling his crimson soaked clothes on a couple of old newspapers then, careful to avoid any of the blood which covered the floor, he moved swiftly out of the kitchen and down to the cellar.

It was cold down there and Edward did not remain there any longer than he had to. He crossed to a cupboard on the far side of the subterranean chamber and pulled the door open. Inside were a pile of large transparent plastic bags he used for wrapping wood to prevent it getting damp and warping. He took out two, closed the cupboard and retreated back to the kitchen.

He wrapped Maureen's body in the two plastic bags, making sure that no blood escaped the polythene covering, but most of it was thick and congealed by now. He dropped the hand in too.

That done, he went to the broom cupboard in the kitchen and took out a mop and bucket, filling the receptacle with hot soapy water.

Then, he set to work.

It was well past three a.m. when he finally dried himself off with the large fluffy towel, watching as the last of the bloodstained water disappeared down the thirsty plughole.

He had spent two hours cleaning up the kitchen, removing every last trace of blood. He had hidden Maureen's body in the room which they had once used as a dining room. The door was now firmly locked. The knife and cleaver had also been cleaned. He had placed a dressing on his nose, relieved to see that the cut hadn't been as bad as he'd first thought. He inspected it again in the bathroom mirror then, pulled the cord and the house was plunged into darkness once more.

He padded across the landing, the towel wrapped around him.

In his hand he held the key, dull but far from rusty. It had not been used for five years.

The key to his parent's room.

He inserted it in the lock and turned it. The hinges creaked protestingly as he entered and Edward made a mental note to oil them, or, better still, put on a new set. He closed the door behind him and stood staring at the bed, a thin smile on his face.

'I said you wouldn't leave me,' he whispered.

On the pillow, leaning against the wall behind, lay the severed head of Maureen. Her blank eyes fixed him in a glassy stare.

Edward smiled and murmured her name once.

Five

Michael Ramsey tapped the end of his pen against the pile of papers on his desk and looked at the wall clock opposite. 10.36 a.m. He looked at his own watch just to double-check. The clacking of typewriters filtered into the office from outside but one, he knew, was silent, its cover still in place.

He got to his feet and wandered out of the office, down the short corridor to the vending machine, passing the two typists on his way. Neither looked up as he passed and Ramsey glanced at the third and vacant typewriter. He thumbed two coins into the vending machine and looked at his watch again. Then, having retrieved his coffee, he made his way back, this time pausing before the two busy secretaries, one of whom stopped typing and looked up at him.

'Has Maureen phoned in today?' he asked.

The girl looked vacant and Ramsey remembered she was only a temp, she would not know all the staff by their first names yet.

'Maureen Briggs,' he amplified.

The second girl looked up, pushing herself back from the machine and the monotonous clacking of keys on paper stopped completely.

'No she hasn't, Mr Ramsey,' she said.

'Thanks,' he said quietly and retreated back into his office.

If Maureen was ill she was not the sort of person to just stay away without phoning to say why she was off. And, he reasoned, if she was unable to get out of bed, she could have asked Edward to do it for her. He tapped his pen again on the papers and looked at the clock for the umpteenth time that morning.

Maureen had been perfectly all right when she left him the previous night.

The coffee tasted bitter in his mouth and he put the plastic cup down.

Where the hell was Maureen?

He waited another five minutes then he reached for the phone.

Edward was half way down the stairs when he heard the phone ringing. He stopped in his tracks, gazing at the object on the small table below him. The strident ringing echoed in the hall and Edward moved slowly down the stairs without taking his eyes off the phone, as if it were some kind of predator that would leap at him when he got close enough to it.

The ringing continued, loud and shrill in the stillness of the house, and Edward reached out a hand, wondering whether to pick up the receiver or not. He eventually decided against it, content to let it ring.

For five minutes solid the high pitched tone filled the house and Edward merely stood watching the instrument until at last, it stopped. He reached forward and took the receiver off the hook, listening to the low burring sound for a moment.

When Michael Ramsey dialled Maureen's number again at three that afternoon he heard the monotonous one tone beeps which would seem to indicate that the phone was engaged.

He tried again at 5.30, just before he left the office. Once more, all he heard were the steady, single notes. He put the receiver down and stroked his chin thoughtfully. Perhaps the line had been engaged both times but he was not convinced.

He took one last look at the phone then left the office, determined to travel to Maureen's house and find out just what was going on.

Six

Ramsey found that the house stood on a slight rise and it seemed to tower above him as he made his way up the street. It stood detached and aloof from the smaller dwellings arranged in neat rows on either side of the road and he thought how incongruous the Briggs' house looked amidst the welter of other buildings. It was a tall dwelling of two storeys but the attic made it seem as if there were an extra floor. The gold light of the dying sun reflected off the single window in the uppermost floor, giving it the appearance of some huge burning eye. Ramsey shuddered involuntarily as the sun behind him darkened and the gold became crimson. It was as if the house would not permit light into its dark confines. As far as he could see, the curtains in the room facing the street were closed but, even at those that were not, the glass seemed to act as a reflector, pushing the unwelcome light away.

The street lights had not yet come on and so he walked along in the twilight, eyes fixed on the gaunt edifice before him. He could understand why Maureen was so anxious to leave this place.

A woman in a house across the street peered from behind her curtains at him, watching as he opened the front gate of the Briggs' house. He saw her looking and waved exaggeratedly. The curtain fell back into place.

Ramsey could smell the creosote which Edward had only recently painted onto the wooden gate and, indeed, as Ramsey pushed it open, some of the black stuff came off on his fingers. He muttered something to himself and pushed the gate shut with his foot. Once again, he paused, looking up at the house which seemed almost menacing from such a close distance. He shook himself, feeling ridiculous, knowing that the prickling at the back of his neck was caused by the icy breeze which had sprung up. He heard something rattling and saw that it was the doors to the cellar bulkhead. His footsteps clicked on the short concrete path and, when he eventually reached the front door he decided to ring the bell.

A two-tone chime sounded and Ramsey waited for it to be answered.

Nothing.

He rang again, his impatience growing somewhat. Nevertheless he waited a little longer. Perhaps Edward or Maureen as in one of the back rooms upstairs.

The door remained firmly closed and, this time, Ramsey used the knocker, slamming it down three times, as hard as he could.

He heard sounds of movement from inside and what appeared to be a bolt being drawn back. Then, the door was opened and he found Edward staring out at him.

'Edward Briggs?' Ramsey said.

Edward nodded, running appraising eyes over this newcomer.

'My name is Michael Ramsey, I was wondering if I could see your sister?'

Edward's face darkened for a fleeting instant but then relaxed. So, this was the man. He forced a smile and nodded, ushering Ramsey inside.

'I don't know if Maureen has spoken to you about me?' said Ramsey, stepping into the hall, blinking hard as the gloom seemed to swallow him. For brief seconds he found it difficult to see anything, but slowly things took on a marked clarity. He saw the staircase to his right, the door to the sitting room before him and another door to the left. It was slightly ajar.

'Sorry, I didn't hear you,' said Edward. 'I was in the cellar.' He nodded towards the half open door on the left. He motioned Ramsey towards the sitting room, pushing the door open for him, flicking the light on.

56

The visitor recoiled once more, this time from the unexpected intrusion of light, but he blinked hard and then turned to face Edward who was still smiling. This was not the reception that Ramsey had expected and he found it more unsettling.

'I'd like to see Maureen,' he said.

'You said you would,' Edward echoed.

'She didn't come to work today, I tried to phone but it was engaged.'

Edward's grin seemed to broaden until it threatened to split his face in two.

'No, it wasn't engaged,' he said, almost proudly. 'I took it off the hook. I was working down in the cellar. I can't hear it when I'm down there anyway so what's the point?' He raised one finger, his eyes widening as if he had suddenly remembered something. 'Excuse me a moment Mr . . .'

'Ramsey.'

'Oh yes, Ramsey.' The smile faded slightly. 'Excuse me while I just shut the cellar door.' He retreated back into the hall, closed the offending door then, swiftly and silently, turned the key in the front entrance. He returned to find Ramsey looking at a photo of Maureen which stood on the TV.

'Maureen told me about you and her,' Edward said, that feral grin returning.

Ramsey nodded.

'Good.' He replaced the photo. 'Is there anything wrong with her? I was worried when she didn't call in this morning.' Ramsey ran his eyes over Edward who was dressed in a stained boiler suit, a screwdriver and hammer jammed into his belt. The hammer dangled by the two wicked, curved claws at the rear of its stainless steel head.

'We still haven't been properly introduced,' said Edward, stepping forward. He extended a grimy hand which Ramsey shook, feeling the strength in the grip. 'I'm Maureen's brother, Edward.'

'She's spoken about you,' Ramsey told him.

'Yes, I suppose she has.'

Ramsey was becoming impatient.

'Look, Mr Briggs, I . . .'

'Edward.'

Ramsey sucked in an agitated breath.

'Edward. I really would like to see Maureen please. We have things to talk about.'

'She told me she was leaving here, to live with you.' That ridiculous grin had vanished and so too, it appeared, had all the colour in Edward's face. Beneath the harsh glow of the light it looked like a skull, the skin stretched tight over thick bones.

'That's right,' Ramsey said, finding that he was anxious to be away from this man. His stomach seemed to have tightened into a fist and he found it difficult to swallow, as if the presence of Edward and the silence in the house were sucking away his strength. He understood how Maureen must have felt, stuck in this house with Edward for five years. It was a wonder she hadn't gone crazy. Crazy. The word stuck in his mind like a knife in wood. Crazy. He looked at Edward again.

'I would like to see Maureen, please,' he said, more forcefully.

'She's upstairs,' said Edward, his grin returning and Ramsey wasn't sure which unsettled him the most. The perpetual leer or the stark blankness. Edward held out a hand, inviting him to follow and, together, they climbed the stairs.

It seemed to get darker the higher they ascended and Ramsey felt that uncomfortable choking feeling come over him once more; he loosened his tie as if it were strangling him. The silence and the gloom clutched even more tightly at him as he followed Edward to one of the four doors which faced them. Ramsey watched as the other man took out a key and unlocked it.

'Why lock the door?' he asked.

'You wanted to see Maureen?' said Edward, pushing the door open.

Ramsey looked at him suspiciously and took a step inside. The curtains were drawn, it was impossible to see.

'The light switch is above you on the right,' Edward told him.

Ramsey flicked it on and the room was bathed in light.

The glow from the fluorescents reflected off the glazed eyes of Maureen's severed head and, for long seconds, Ramsey was transfixed by the sight. His jaw dropped open, his lips fluttering soundlessly. He felt his stomach begin to churn and, with a grunt, he fell against the open door, eyes still fixed on the hacked-off appendage.

He heard the arc of the hammer as Edward brought it down.

The blunt head caught Ramsey above the right ear, cracking his skull. He staggered drunkenly and tried to avoid the second blow but it was useless. His face a mask of fury, Edward struck again and stove in part of Ramsey's forehead. Blood burst from the hole and the other man dropped to his knees, arms raised in a vain attempt to shield himself.

Edward spun the hammer, using the sharp claws to lash at his helpless victim. The steel bit into Ramsey's arm and, as Edward tore it free, it ripped away part of his forearm and the material of his sleeve. Ramsey shrieked in pain, his head bursting from the two wounds he had already received but, somehow, he clung to consciousness.

Edward gritted his teeth, his face now scarlet with rage. He brought the twin claws down once more and, this time, they pierced Ramsey's skull, tearing into his cranial cavity and as he fell forward, the hammer was actually pulled from Edward's hand, still embedded in his opponent's head. Ramsey's body was twitching, a combination of muscle spasm and genuine movement. Edward grabbed the rubber handle of the tool and tugged, physically dragging his dying victim several feet across the landing until, with a surge of demonic strength, he wrenched the recalcitrant hammer free. There was a strident crack of breaking bone followed by a vile sucking sound as a large portion of Ramsey's skull and some sticky brain matter were torn away. A flux of blood and clear fluid spilled onto the landing, puddling around his head.

Edward stood over the body for long seconds, glaring down at it then he crossed to the door of the bedroom, noticing that some blood had splashed up onto the paintwork. He shut the door, making a mental note to clean the blood off later. There was more of it on the landing, as well as pieces of silvery-grey slime which looked like congealed porridge. Edward kicked Ramsey's body and his hand moved spasmodically.

Edward smiled.

The cleaning up would have to wait.

He lifted the other man's body onto his shoulders and headed down the stairs towards the cellar.

Edward was naked but, despite the chill air in the cellar he appeared unperturbed.

He looked at the body of Ramsey, also naked. It lay on the work bench and, as Edward watched, the dying man moaned softly, the fingers of his left hand flexing weakly. His eyes remained closed, one of them at least, sealed by the congealed blood which had pumped down from the hole in his forehead.

Edward pressed the red button on the chainsaw and the McCullough roared into life. He moved towards the prone form of his victim, slowly lowering the monstrous blade towards the other man's stomach.

He drove it into the soft flesh, ignoring the blood which spattered into his face, whipped by the churning hooks on the rapidly turning chain. The tool sliced through skin, muscle and entrails with ease, not even slowing as it met Ramsey's sternum.

Edward could hear another sound above the high pitched roar of the chainsaw and, it took him a moment to realize that it was his own maniacal shouting. He cursed and screamed at Ramsey as he drew the McCullough back and forth across the body which jerked with each fresh incision. The chest cavity was open, gaping wide as if it had been prized apart by giant pliers. The savage spinning chain hacked through both lungs which collapsed like burst balloons, expelling a foul smelling gas and thick gouts of blood as they did so. Edward felt the erection throbbing between his legs as he continued to hack away at the corpse and, when he finally switched the chainsaw off, in the silence which descended, he could hear his own excited guttural breathing.

For what seemed like an eternity he gazed at what was left of Michael Ramsey then, he crossed to one of the cupboards and removed a polythene bag, the same type he had used to put Maureen's body in. He lifted the eviscerated corpse onto his shoulder for the second time that night and carried it up the cellar steps, his bare feet leaving bloodied marks as he trudged through the house to the dining room. He unlocked the door and went in.

Maureen's body was where he had left it the previous night, propped up against the door of a large cupboard, ordinarily used for storing crockery. He had removed the plates earlier in the day, they stood stacked nearby. Edward first pushed his sister's headless corpse into the cupboard and then lifted Ramsey's body, pushing it on top of her, using his foot to ensure that both bodies were secure in their make-shift resting place.

He closed the cupboard doors and left the dining room, locking it behind him.

Once more, he was tired but, this time he felt a peculiar kind of exhilaration as well.

He went into the kitchen and retrieved the mop and bucket.

Seven

The police arrived about ten o'clock the following morning. A panda car drew up before the house and a tall, thin-faced constable got out, checking the number. He nodded to his colleague who clambered out of the car and followed his companion up the short path to the front door.

Edward saw them coming.

He was already at the bottom of the stairs when the two tone chime sounded in the stifling confines of the hall.

He opened the door, his face impassive.

'Mr Edward Briggs?' said the taller and older of the two men.

He nodded.

'Come in.' His tone was solemn, but he tried to smile as he led them to the sitting room.

'My name is P.C. Weeks,' said the taller man. He motioned to his companion. 'This is Constable Hughes.'

Edward smiled thinly again.

'I'm sorry to have to trouble you,' he said.

'It's no trouble, Mr Briggs,' Weeks told him. 'When exactly did your sister leave here?' The policeman took out a notebook.

'Yesterday, no, sorry, the day before,' said Edward. 'I can't understand what's happened. Anything could have happened to her.'

'Do you and your sister live here together?' asked Weeks, scribbling as Edward spoke.

'Yes, we have done since our parents . . . died, five years ago.' He exhaled deeply, sniffing a little. The ruse appeared to be working because Weeks asked him if he

62

were feeling all right. 'I'm sorry, Constable. I just want to know what's happened to her.'

'Probably nothing has happened to her, Mr Briggs,' said the older man reassuringly. 'Now, I just need some details, a description and a photo if you have one, please.'

He chose the one from the top of the TV set, watching as Weeks slipped it from the frame. He took particulars about her age, where she worked and anything else he could think of. Finally he flipped the notebook shut.

Hughes, standing beside Edward reached for his two-way radio as it crackled into life. He spoke into it then apologised to Edward, telling Weeks that he was going back to the car. The older man waited until he heard the front door close then looked first at the photo and then Edward.

'Can you think of any reason why your sister would want to leave home?' he asked.

Edward shook his head, the lie ready on his tongue.

'She was so happy here, we both were,' he said. 'After the death of our parents we became closer, so to speak.'

'Did she have any boyfriends?' asked the policeman.

Edward paused, rubbing his hands together in mock nervousness.

'There was a man,' he said. 'I don't know what his name is. She'd been seeing him for quite a time.'

'And you knew about this?'

'Oh yes, I was pleased for her. I'd told her myself that she should find someone, that she shouldn't rely on me all the time.'

'So why does it surprise you that she might have gone off with this man?'

Edward swallowed hard, the question taking him a little by surprise.

'As I said, she was happy here. There was no reason for her to leave.' His voice had lost some of its false solemnity.

Weeks studied his features carefully.

'Was she in love with this man?' he asked.

'They *were* lovers if that's what you mean,' Edward told him.

63

'Had she told you that?'

'I assumed it.'

Edward realized that his trick was in danger of failing.

'She took all her clothes,' he said. 'Come and look in her bedroom. She took everything.' He got to his feet.

'That won't be necessary, Mr Briggs,' Weeks told him.

'How long before I'll know anything?' Edward asked.

The policeman shrugged.

'That's difficult to say, we'll have to check hospitals first.'

Edward looked horrified.

'It's standard procedure, Mr Briggs.' The constable took a piece of paper from his pocket and handed it to Edward who scanned the sheet. It was an official report, which required the missing person's name and address to be filled in. He did so dutifully, signing his own name at the bottom. He handed the form back to Weeks. The policeman made his way to the front door, followed by Edward.

'Please find her,' he said, the practised concern back in his voice.

Weeks nodded.

'It's very quiet here isn't it?' he said, the silence crowding in on him.

'My father soundproofed the house himself,' said Edward. 'He hated noise.'

Weeks smiled again and allowed Edward to open the front door for him. 'We'll be in touch as soon as we hear anything,' he said.

Edward waited until the policeman was half-way down the path and then called after him.

'Please find her.'

He closed the front door and lay against it, a thin film of perspiration sheathing his body, his rasping breaths loud in the solitude but, after a few moments, he chuckled and the low sniggers gradually grew into full-bodied laughter.

* * *

Hughes saw his colleague close the gate behind him and cross the pavement to the car. As Weeks slid into the passenger seat the younger man looked at him.

'Well,' he said.

Weeks appeared puzzled.

'Well, what?' he said.

'What did he say?'

The older man repeated the conversation, kneading the bridge of his nose between thumb and forefinger as he did so.

'Well, it's bloody obvious what's happened isn't it?' said Hughes when his colleague had finished. 'She's buggered off with her boyfriend.'

'That's what I thought,' Weeks confessed. 'But the poor sod is pretty cut up all the same. You'd think it was his wife that had hopped it, not his sister. Still, we'd better go through the motions, we might run something up. Come on, let's get on with it.'

Hughes reached for the ignition key but then hesitated, looking past Weeks towards the house. He snapped his fingers.

'You know I knew there was something familiar about this gaff when we arrived,' he said.

'I'm not with you.'

'Don't you remember the case? A bloke sliced up his old woman then cut his throat. It happened in that house. When Briggs said his parents had been dead for five years I thought I was right. His father was Ralph Briggs, the bloke who killed his Mrs and then topped himself.'

'No wonder the sister left home,' said Weeks, glancing at the house once more. 'Come on.'

This time Hughes did start the car.

Watching from the sitting room, Edward saw the panda pull away.

Eight

'He's dead, Maureen. He would have taken you from me and I couldn't allow that.'

Edward knelt at the end of the bed, gazing at the head of his sister. Even though it had only been there for three days, the severed appendage was beginning to show signs of degeneration. The cheeks were sunken and hollow, the flesh hanging in places. The eyes themselves had dulled and were on the way to becoming opaque. The whites were heavily tinged with yellow, as if stained by nicotine. The bloodless lips were still drawn back in a rictus but the tongue that protruded from between them was bloated and dark. Like some swollen, bulbous leech. There were pieces of fluff on its dry surface.

The room had begun to smell, a thick, rank odour which reminded Edward of rotting fish.

He knelt in the darkness, as if he were in church, worshipping before some kind of obscene shrine.

'The police asked me why you wanted to leave,' he said, softly. 'I told them about *him*.' He emphasised the last word with disgust. 'He came here last night. He wanted you. And you would have gone with him wouldn't you?' He clenched his teeth. 'You would have left me for *him*. Wouldn't you?' He roared the last two words, the veins at his temples throbbing angrily.

And now the tone of his voice had changed, it was bitter, hurt almost.

'Didn't I mean anything to you? It would have been easy for you to walk out wouldn't it? I suppose *he* was everything that I am not. *He* could give you things that I couldn't.'

Then, as quickly as it had erupted, Edward's anger seemed to subside.

'I love you as much as he did. *More* than he did. More than he ever could.'

He got to his feet, no longer the suppliant asking for reciprocation of his feelings. His anger this time was boundless.

'How could he even know how to love you?' he roared. 'And yet you would have left me alone for *him*. Do you know what I did to him? I cut him up. I gutted him like the pig he is. And I enjoyed it too.' He smiled crookedly. 'You thought he could give you everything didn't you? *He* was the one you wanted to live with for the rest of your life. And why? Because he was good in bed? Because he could satisfy you?'

He stared at the severed skull, his own eyes fixed on those opaque orbs now sunken in their sockets. The eyelids were swollen, the right upper lid little more than a useless flap which was beginning to cover part of the eye.

'You wanted to leave me,' Edward gasped, sucking in lungfuls of stale air. 'All I ever did was love you. I always will.'

He leant forward towards the head, pressing his own warm lips against the bloodless, cold ones of Maureen. He tasted the rankness on his tongue, smelt the vile odour clogging in his nostrils but, when he finally broke away, his expression was unchanged.

He ran one hand through the lank, matted hair and smiled crookedly.

Nine

Dave Todd pulled up the collar of his leather jacket and dug his free hand into his pocket. With the other he pushed the remains of the hamburger into his mouth and wiped the grease off on his jeans. He banged his heels against the wall, stamping them hard in an effort to restore the circulation. Despite the fact that he was standing in the doorway of a boarded-up shop, the harsh wind was still whipping along the street, ruffling his hair and numbing his ears.

'Shit,' he muttered, scanning the scene before him.

Across the wide road, amidst the welter of people moving backwards and forwards, stood two girls. Both were in their twenties, one – the taller of the two – had short blonde hair which was held firmly in place by half a can of lacquer. She wore a leather mini skirt and thigh length boots, topped by a silky blouse which seemed to change colour according to the hue of the flashing neon lights which were sparkling behind her. Her hair, doused with so much lacquer, sparkled as much as the lights. She was shivering, Todd could see that even from his position across the street.

So too was her companion. A girl with shoulder-length brown hair which grew thickly, plastered across her face periodically by the strong breeze. She was dressed in a tight red T-shirt against which her large nipples strained, coaxed to points by the chill wind. She too wore a mini skirt but her legs were unfettered by boots, ending instead with a pair of white, high-heeled ankle straps which only further enhanced the smooth curve of her calves and the strong suppleness of her thighs. They were both standing outside a club, the blonde sucking on a cigarette.

As Todd watched, a car pulled up by the curb and the

blonde girl walked across to it. He saw the driver wind down his window and gesture a couple of times, then he wound the window up again and drove off. The blonde retreated back to her position outside the club.

Todd scuttled across the road and headed towards them.

'Well, if it isn't Rupert Murdoch again,' said the blonde, smiling. 'Where you been hiding this time?'

He pointed out his vantage point.

'How are you, lover boy?' the blonde asked him.

'Cold,' Todd told her. He turned to her brown haired companion. 'How are you, Vicki?' he said, smiling.

'I'm OK, Dave,' she said.

'You got any more bleeding' fags?' the blonde asked him. 'I've run out.'

Todd rummaged in his pocket and found a half-empty packet of Rothmans which he gave to the girl. She was twenty-three, two years younger than her brown-haired companion and seven younger than Todd himself. Her name was Penny Dawson. At least that was the name everyone knew her by, whether it was her real name or not was still a mystery. But then, London was full of mysteries Todd had discovered.

'Any action about tonight?' he asked.

Vicki Powell shook her head.

'It's too cold. not every punter's got a car and some of them don't fancy walking to the house from here. Not in this weather anyway.'

'Did you see that geezer just then?' she asked Todd.

He nodded.

'He wanted to pay a fiver for a bleedin' half and half. I told him to sod off. What's he think I am? A bloody charity?' She sucked hard on her cigarette, swallowing the smoke.

Todd looked at Vicki, trying not to, but unable to prevent himself studying her figure.

She noticed his interested gaze and smiled.

'Either of you fancy a coffee?' he asked.

'We're working girls you know,' said Penny. 'We can't

just go swanning off with handsome reporters when we feel like it. Besides, if Joe finds out I've left me patch he won't be very pleased. Greedy little bastard.'

'I'll come with you, Dave,' Vicki told him.

The two of them wandered off, turning to watch as Penny approached another car which had pulled up by the kerb, This time they saw her nod her head and, just before she clambered into the passenger seat, she looked across at them and gave a thumbs-up signal.

Vicki laughed.

'Well, she'll be OK for the night.'

The two of them walked on, past clubs and cinemas, past pubs where music came blasting out of open doors to mingle with the sound of traffic. The pavement seemed to change colour as scores of neon lights burned in the night, dazzling the eye. The air hummed with energy. Soho had come to life with the onset of night, like some kind of nocturnal hunter it had slumbered during the daylight hours, waiting for the darkness before it gained full power.

The narrow streets and alleys were thronged with people, moving agitatedly about. Others strolled as if on a sight-seeing trip. Vicki nodded greetings to a number of people, as did Todd, for during the past two weeks he too had come to know the denizens of Soho. He was working on a series of articles about vice for *The Herald*, a paper he had worked for these past ten years. He had been to Soho before but he had never seen what really went on in the dirtiest and saddest area of the capital. The trade in sex, where human beings were commodities to be bought and sold, was miserable. There was little happiness and certainly no comfort to be found in this shadow city.

Todd himself had been brought up in Bermondsey so he was no stranger to the harsher side of life, but during his years on the paper he had seen things which had shocked even him. Most of those he had witnessed in the past two weeks. The paper had booked him into the Venus Hotel in Shaftsbury Avenue and, in the early hours of the morning, he retreated to his single room and typed up the notes which he had made during the day and night. He wrote about the pimps, the whores, the massage parlours, the porno cinemas, the bookshops. The list was endless and each carried with it that feeling of sadness. And waste.

He looked at Vicki, barely twenty-five, and wondered just why the hell she continued living as she did. It was a question he had not yet got around to asking her. They had grown close over the last fortnight, perhaps a little too close. Todd felt a strong affection for her, tinged with pity. She too was attracted to the journalist, but the nature of her work enabled her to retain a buffer between what she showed towards him and what she actually felt for him. However, she too realized that she was fighting a losing battle. Todd's rugged appearance and gentle manner aroused her in a way she thought she had lost. When she looked at other men she saw merely customers, but when she looked at Todd she saw something more.

They walked until they came to a small café, its windows steamy despite the fact that the door was open. Vicki walked in first and sat down at a table near to the door. It was hot inside the café, great clouds of steam issuing from the huge tea urn which stood at one end of the counter. Behind it stood a large man in a white overall. It was spotted with stains of all descriptions and Todd had to suppress a snigger as the image of a walking menu sprang to mind. He could picture the man pointing to each stain and saying 'Well, there's this, this or this.' He pushed the image to the back of his mind and ordered two coffees, scanning the interior of the café as he waited for the man to pour them.

There were two girls sitting in one corner of the building chatting animatedly to a coloured chap who was constantly fiddling with his cuff links.

Beside them, a group of youths with mohican hair cuts were drinking tea through straws and laughing raucously. One of them glanced across at Todd who met the boy's gaze without wavering, only turning away when the man behind the counter pushed the two coffees across to him, slopping most of one into the saucer. Todd gave him the money and returned to the table where Vicki sat, examining her make-up in the mirror she'd taken from her hand bag. She thanked Todd for the coffee and he sipped his tentatively, wincing at the taste.

'So, how much longer are you going to be around?' Vicki asked, running a hand through her hair.

Todd shrugged.

'Another week, maybe more. Why?'

'Just curious,' she said, and reached for her coffee.

He studied her features, allowing his eyes to stray briefly to her small breasts. She had a small scar just above the left one, visible because her T-shirt was cut so low.

'How did you get that scar?' he asked her.

'Which one?' she said.

'There's more than one?' he enquired, surprised.

She nodded.

'Aren't you going to ask me how I got them? It's your job to ask questions isn't it?'

'OK,' he said. 'How did you get them?'

She pointed to the one on her breast.

'I got that one and the other ones on my tit from a john. He did it with a knife. Nothing serious, thank Christ, or I'd have been no good to anybody. I mean, who wants a bitch with sliced-up tits?'

'What the hell was he doing with a knife?' asked Todd.

'He was a freak,' she explained. 'He wanted to play at rape. It was the only way he could get off.'

'You said there were other scars.'

She nodded.

'Danny gave me those,' she said.

'The bastard. Why?'

'I turned down a really expensive trick. Two Arabs wanted to play Russian roulette with me. One of them held the gun against my fanny, at least that's what he wanted to do. The other one wanted me to suck him off while his friend was doing it. I told them to sod off. Danny belted me around for that. They would have payed two hundred quid for that.'

72

Todd shook his head.

'Jesus Christ. Why the hell do you stay with him if he treats you badly?'

'I've got nowhere else to go,' she said.

'I thought a pimp was supposed to look after his girls, not knock them about.'

'Pimps couldn't give a shit as long as their girls are bringing in the money. We're expendable, Dave, you should know that, you've seen how this game operates. There's always plenty more waiting to take your place.'

He stared down into the bottom of his cup and then up at Vicki who was lighting up a cigarette. The smell of smoke mingled with the odour of greasy onions which were frying on the hot plate behind the counter.

'Why did you start, Vicki?' he asked.

She smiled.

'I was wondering when you were going to ask me that. It's taken you two weeks.'

'Surely there must have been other things you could have done. Anything's better than this.'

'People always think there's some kind of psychological explanation for why a girl goes on the game. Broken home, rough childhood, that sort of thing. Most of the girls working these streets, working any streets, are doing it because they've got no choice. It's easy money and that's not something you come by very often. Some of them enjoy it. Penny does.' Vicki sipped the last bitter dregs of her coffee. 'Me. I've been on the game for four years, before that I was a stripper. My parents threw me out when I was sixteen, I had nowhere to go. I didn't know anybody. London's a terrific place if you've got friends but when you're on your own it's the worst place in the world. What would you have done in my position?'

He exhaled deeply.

'I don't know,' he confessed.

'There's a lot of men in the same position. You've seen them yourself. There's nearly as many blokes working the streets as women.'

'But I'm talking about *you*,' he said and their eyes locked. 'You're a very attractive girl. You're intelligent. You don't belong here.'

'And who's going to take care of me if I leave?' she asked. 'Am I just going to become a house-wife? A kept woman?' She chuckled but there was bitterness in her tone. 'I'm to be used, Dave, nothing more. How many blokes would want to know me if they found out what I'd been?'

'So what's it going to take to get you away from this?' he asked exasperatedly.

'The love of a good man,' she said, sarcastically.

'Don't bullshit me, Vicki. I'm serious.'

'Why worry yourself? It's not worth it.'

'*I* think it is.'

She coloured slightly, knowing that he meant it.

'Thanks.' When she spoke it came out as a low whisper.

'Just think about it, at least do that for me,' he asked. 'Think about giving up the game.'

She nodded, her brown eyes fixing him in a soft stare.

'I don't think I'd know how to cope with a proper relationship,' she said.

'You'd manage,' he told her. .

'With the right kind of help.'

He nodded.

'What about you?' she said. 'Could you care for someone like me? Knowing what I am, what I've done?'

'Yes,' he said, unhesitatingly.

She swallowed hard and got to her feet.

'Well, for now, I'd better get back to work. Danny won't be very pleased if I go home empty-handed.'

Todd remained seated, watching as she straightened her clothes.

'Think about what I've said,' he murmured.

She bent and kissed his forehead then, she was gone. Todd sat alone at the table, watching as streams of condensation ran down the window like grimy tears.

* * *

It was almost 1.35 a.m. when Vicki returned to the house in Earlham street which she had shared with Danny Foster and three other girls for the last five years. As she closed the door behind her, Foster emerged from a room to the left of the hallway. He was a short man, stockily built and dressed in just the trousers and waist-coat of an old pin stripe suit. His skin was tinted and, when he spoke, his voice was thick with accent. That which had earned him his name of 'Maltese Danny'.

'Where the fuck have you been?' he said, irritably, retreating into the other room.

Vicki followed him. She sat down, gazing at the piles of money which were stacked on the coffee table before him. There was a half empty can of lager there too and some empties strewn beneath.

'Well, hand it over,' Foster snapped, holding out a hand which sported bitten-down, filthy fingernails and a long scar.

Vicki took some money from her bag, handed it to the pimp and watched as he counted it.

'Twenty-five fucking quid,' he rasped. 'What the hell is this supposed to be? Where's the rest?'

'There isn't any more, Danny. You were lucky to get that.'

'Yeah? Well you better do more than this tomorrow or I'll kick your fucking arse.' He glared at her. 'I'm trying to run a business.'

'It's not my fault,' she protested, wearily. 'That was one straight, a hand job and a special. What do you want, miracles?'

He turned on her vehemently.

'No I want you to keep away from that fucking reporter.'

She looked surprised.

'I haven't seen him today, I . . .'

He cut her short.

'Don't fuck with me, girl. You think I don't hear things? You were in Frank's place with him tonight. I was told. Nothing goes on in this place without me knowing about it.

75

Now I'm telling you to stay away from him. I don't like people sticking their nose into my affairs and I don't want him screwing up my business. Got it?'

She got to her feet.

'I'm going to bed,' she told him.

He grabbed her arm as she passed, squeezing her wrist hard.

'Keep away from him, right?' he growled.

She tugged free and left the room, climbing the darkened stairway to the landing. She went into the bathroom and took a quick shower then, with a towel wrapped around her, clutching her clothes and handbag, she retreated to the bedroom which she shared with another girl. Vicki moved around as quietly as she could, glancing every now and then at the sleeping form in the bed next to her own.

'Vicki.'

The voice startled her.

'I'm sorry,' she said. 'I didn't mean to wake you up.'

Amy Curtis sat up, reaching for the switch on the bedside lamp. The sixty watt bulb filled the room with a warm glow.

'I wasn't asleep,' said Amy, her voice still carrying the slight Scots lilt which Vicki found so fascinating. She was younger than Vicki, yet to reach her twenty-first birthday. She, like so many other girls of her age, had left Scotland expecting to find work in London but had found that the streets were paved not with gold but with shit. She had been a prostitute for two years. She swung herself out of bed, her long black hair flowing over her breasts and shoulders.

Vicki had seated herself before the large mirror on the dressing table and was busily drying her hair.

'Can I help?' asked Amy, smiling and Vicki handed her the towel, allowing the younger girl to rub her brown locks. When she had finished drying it, Amy reached for the brush which lay nearby and set about the task of running it through Vicki's thick hair. The older girl closed her eyes, the movements relaxing her.

'That Danny's a bastard,' she said, and proceeded to tell Amy of their argument.

76

The Scots girl continued with her brushing, kissing the top of Vicki's head when she'd finished. She felt soft hands on her shoulders, kneading expertly, loosening muscles which felt as tight as drawn wire. Amy gently stroked Vicki's neck, gripping the flesh tighter as she moved down the older girl's shoulders.

Vicki sighed contentedly and allowed her head to loll back as the soft hands found their way to her breasts, squeezing and kneading gently, thumbs outlining the nipples which stiffened and grew to hard peaks. She opened her legs slightly, the warm feeling between them gradually turning to liquid desire as Amy's hands moved more urgently on her body. The Scots girl found that her own body felt hot, her own breasts tight, her own cleft now moist. She moved in front of Vicki, allowing the older girl to begin her own probings and it was Amy's turn to gasp as Vicki's searching fingers began to stroke her clitoris, rubbing gently for precious moments before slipping deeper into the hot liquescence of her vagina. Vicki felt her companions hand sliding down her belly and she eagerly allowed Amy's expert fingers to infiltrate her slippery cleft.

They remained like that for long moments, enjoying the pleasure which they received and also which they gave until, finally, they moved across to one of the beds and fingers were replaced by tongues. The excitement grew until it finally peaked as both of them reached orgasm, their bodies racked by waves of pleasure which they were unfamiliar with during their working hours. The two of them lay together, talking softly, then Amy retreated to her own bed and both of them settled down to sleep.

Amy drifted easily into oblivion but Vicki lay for a long time, listening to the gradually diminishing sounds of traffic from outside. Staring at the ceiling and then at the walls where pieces of paper were beginning to peel away like leprous skin.

She wondered what Todd was doing.

Ten

Edward turned the key in the bedroom door, pausing a moment on the threshold. He wrinkled his nose and winced. The smell had definitely got worse since the last time. He pushed the door to behind him and walked across to the foot of the bed, staring at the severed head of his sister, still propped up on the pillow by the wall.

The skin was the colour of rancid butter and, it had taken on a waxy appearance. The eyes seemed even more sunken in their sockets, the lids now flaps of wrinkled flesh. The tongue, which continued to protrude from between the bloodless lips, was now almost black. The skin around the stump of the neck was mottled purple in places, signalling the onset of gangrene. One tendril-like vein was shrivelled up like burnt hair.

Edward studied the head carefully, pulling at his shirt collar. It felt tight around his neck and that, combined with the choking atmosphere inside the room, made him feel as if he were being strangled. He thought about loosening his tie but decided against it.

'I'm going out,' he said to the empty air. 'The way you used to. When you used to leave me alone at nights to be with *him*.' Edward's voice was low but full of anger.

'I told you my time would come and it has. All these years I remained faithful to *you*.' He glared at the head as if expecting it to answer him. 'I loved *you*, no one else meant anything to me. I trusted you but you betrayed that trust.' His voice turned reflective. 'Why is it that women have no understanding of trust? Why is it that they cannot see when a man loves them? Why couldn't *you* see how much I loved you?' His anger returned swiftly. 'Well, now *I* am going to

78

find someone else, as you did. You never cared for me, so what I am going to do is not betrayal.' He paused. 'Even if it was, I'd still be in my rights to do it. Even after what you did to me, I love you. But, for all these years I haven't even looked at another woman, but now I'm going to find one and I'll bring her here.' He grinned crookedly. 'I might even fuck her in front of you. I'm as much a man as *he* ever was.'

Edward glared at the head a moment longer then he turned and left the room, closing the door behind him. He left the key in the lock but he did not turn it.

As he reached the bottom of the stairs he glanced at himself in the hall mirror, smoothing down a patch of hair which had sprung up above his left ear. Then, satisfied with his appearance, he stepped out into the night.

Eleven

The drive across London took Edward about forty minutes. He drove slowly, gazing around at the explosions of multi-coloured neon lights which seemed to burst from every shop front and cinema hoarding. Despite the fact that it was after ten o'clock, many shops were still open and he saw people milling about both inside and also on the pavements. So intent was he on watching a young couple in a disused shop doorway that he forgot just how slowly he was driving. The youngsters stood in a corner doorway as if wedged there and, quite oblivious to the amused stares of passers-by, the man was eagerly pushing his hand up beneath the girl's skirt. Edward was shocked from his own observations by the blast of a car horn behind him and he turned to see a taxi pull out and overtake him, the driver gesturing angrily.

Edward drove on.

Two men lay beside a phone box, each clutching a bottle, while their companion used the booth as a urinal, happily emptying his bladder inside the box.

Further up the same street, a woman was being ejected from a club by a large doorman who pushed her from the entrance with such force she nearly rolled into the road. She got to her feet screaming abuse at the man who merely laughed until the woman hawked loudly and spat in his face. As Edward watched, the doorman drew back his left hand and, with one powerful blow, pole-axed the woman. He left her lying on the pavement and went back inside the club. People passing were careful to step over the prone body of the woman.

Lights flashed frenziedly, all the colours of the rainbow. Some of them spelling out words. Edward read:

TOPLESS WAITRESSES
PEEP SHOW
UNCENSORED 16mm FILMS

He managed to find a parking space and slipped the Dolomite between a Capri and a large American car. He locked the door and gazed around him. There were women, young and old, walking about, standing talking. Some alone, some in twos. They chatted to each other, to the men who passed by and, more than once, Edward saw one stop a man. He watched, a mixture of fascination and disgust etched on his face. The man eventually led the woman to a waiting car and Edward watched as they drove off. He turned and walked slowly up the street where he was parked, eyes scanning everything around him. A cinema nearby was showing something called 'Sex School' and Edward paused to look at the posters outside. One of them showed a girl dressed in a school uniform bending over a desk while a naked man hit her with a cane. Edward wondered why there was black tape across the place where the man's genitals should have been. He walked on, past a club which boasted 'Four different girls on stage every hour'.

He swallowed hard and peered at the entrance which seemed to consist solely of long platted lengths of multi-coloured plastic. He could hear music coming from inside, a throbbing rhythm which seemed to make the pavement itself shudder.

'Only two quid, guvnor.'

Edward stepped back in surprise as the man emerged from the darkness inside the doorway.

He looked at Edward and smiled, revealing a row of brown teeth.

'Two quid. Four different girls every hour on stage,' he said, proudly. 'Just two quid.'

Edward shook his head and moved away, glancing back at the man with brown teeth.

'Only two quid,' the man called after him then retreated

back into the darkness. Edward walked on, gazing up at a shop front which read:

LOVETIME

It was a book shop and, through the open door, he could see perhaps half a dozen men inside browsing through the numerous magazines which filled the shelves. Edward stepped inside. The man behind the counter looked up briefly. He was broad, the T-shirt he wore bearing the legend: Live for Fun, Loyal to none. Thick brown hair cascaded over his muscular shoulders which looked as though they would, at any second, burst the material of his shirt. He was eating a hot dog and reading a magazine. Edward paused before the counter, his attention attracted by the video recorder which was propped on one end. There was a TV set there, too, and he stood mesmerised, watching as a white woman was tied down by three coloured men dressed as Zulus. As Edward watched, all three men stripped off and took it in turns to have sex with the woman. Finally he turned and began scanning the shelves. Dozens of glossy faces pouted back at him and Edward took one of the magazines down, flipping through it. He noticed that there were some in polythene wrappers.

The banks of fluorescents blazed coldly overhead, their light reflecting off the glossy pages of the magazines which he held. He went through four of the magazines before finally wandering back out onto the street again. The youth behind the counter glanced up again as Edward left then returned to the more immediate task of finishing his hot dog.

As Edward glanced back down the street he saw that someone was leaning on the bonnet of his car.

He frowned and began walking towards the vehicle, noticing, as he drew closer, that it was a woman. She was dressed in a leather coat, worn at the elbows, which concealed a black skirt and flimsy blouse. There was another, younger girl, with her dressed in a thin sweater,

82

tight black trousers and knee boots. Both of them looked up as Edward approached.

The one leaning on the bonnet, older with blonde hair, smiled at Edward.

'You're leaning on my car,' he said, running appraising eyes over the blonde. She wore a gold cross around her neck and it nestled between her breasts, sparkling invitingly when the light struck it.

Penny Dawson stepped forward and pretended to brush some imaginary dirt from the place where she'd been sitting.

'Pardon me, love,' she said.

Edward looked at the other girl who also smiled. But, behind that smile, Amy Curtis was wondering whether they had found a punter or not.

'Are you looking for someone?' she asked him.

'We saw you come out of that shop,' said Penny. 'Why look at books when you can have the real thing, eh?' She chuckled and Edward felt himself colour. But, the warmth which flushed his face was more anger than embarrassment. He looked at the blonde, eyes narrowed.

'What's your name?' Penny asked him.

'Briggs,' he told her. 'Edward Briggs.'

'All right then, *Eddie*,' said Penny, grinning. 'What are you doing here? If you want someone to show you around . . .' She allowed the sentence to trail off.

He looked more closely at her. At the eye shadow, put on so thick it made her look as if someone had given her a beating, at the sticky red lipstick, the pitted cheeks covered with rouge and her hair, held in place by so much lacquer. The sight disgusted him but, at the same time aroused him.

'How much?' he asked, unflinchingly.

Penny smiled again.

'That depends.'

'How much if you spend the night with me?'

She shook her head.

'Sorry, love, I never spend the night with punters, I . . .'

Her words seemed to fade as he reached into his pocket

and produced a wad of ten pound notes as thick as an index finger.

'How much?' he said again.

'Fifty quid,' she told him. 'But anything else is extra.'

He nodded and opened the car door for her.

Amy looked at Penny and then at Edward.

'Penny . . .' she began to protest.

'Forget it, Amy,' Penny whispered. 'This john's loaded. So what if he likes the comfort of home.'

Edward slid into the car beside her and started the engine.

'My friend could come along too,' Penny told him. 'We can do a little number for you if that's what you like.'

He looked at her and shook his head.

'Just you,' he murmured, icily, and pulled out.

Amy watched the car drive off. What the hell did Penny think she was up to? None of the girls ever went home with punters, that was one of their own rules. But, Penny didn't seem to care and, after all, the man *had* been loaded. Amy herself had seen the stack of tenners. Penny might pull in a ton for her night's work. Or more. Even so, as Amy watched the Dolomite disappear into the traffic, she felt the hairs rise on the back of her neck. But why she couldn't say.

Twelve

Edward parked the car in the driveway and got out, leading Penny to the front door. She had chattered inanely throughout the entire journey while he had merely sat, eyes fixed on the road ahead. Once, she had placed her hand on his thigh, rubbing his crutch until she felt his stiffness beneath her fingers but now, as he opened the front door to let her in, he watched her with eyes full of contempt not desire.

She wandered into the hall, her high heels clicking loudly in the silence.

'Bleedin' hell, it's quiet here isn't it?' she exclaimed.

He nodded and motioned her into the sitting room.

She walked ahead of him, eyes scanning the large room.

'Do you live here on your own?' she asked.

'I live with my sister.'

Penny raised her eyebrows.

'Very cosy,' she said. 'Right, what's it going to be then?'

Edward look puzzled, watching her as she sat down, crossing her legs to reveal her thighs.

'How do you want to spend your money?' she told him. 'Straight. Half and half. Blow job.' She paused. 'If you're into S and M or anything else heavy it'll cost you extra, on top of the fifty you're paying me to stay the night.'

'I still don't understand,' he said.

'Christ, love, where have you been hiding for the last thirty years?' she asked, mockingly. 'A straight will cost you another tenner. Half and half is twenty-five, a blow job's fifteen. Anything else is another fifty.'

He looked at her, running his eyes over her scantily clad form.

'Half and half?' he murmured.

'Yeah, suck and fuck. Right?'

He nodded.

She got to her feet.

'So, where do you want it? Down here. In the bedroom? You're paying, it's up to you.'

'Upstairs,' he said and led her out of the sitting room.

As they climbed the steps Penny wrinkled her nose. 'What's that smell?' she asked. 'It's like something rotten.'

He didn't speak.

'You don't say much do you, love? Still no one says you have to. You can do it with a bag over your head if you like.' She chuckled.

They reached the landing and Edward ushered her towards his bedroom. She walked in and, as he flicked on the light, she began to remove her clothes. He stood in the doorway, watching as she kicked off her shoes, simultaneously unbuttoning her blouse to reveal her breasts. She glanced up and saw him gazing at her.

'You like to watch do you?' she said and slowed the pace of her undressing, slipping the zip on her skirt down and pulling the garment free. Beneath it she wore no panties and Edward ran his eyes over her naked form, grinning slightly at the contrast between the bright blonde of her hair and the dark patch of triangular curls between her legs. She lay back on the bed, running both hands over her body, teasing her nipples until they grew stiff, allowing one index finger to slip through that maze of pubic hair and part her outer lips.

He watched impassively, his own excitement growing, and he began to undress, finally standing naked beside her, his penis throbbing, his heart hammering madly against his ribs. He stood there shaking, watching as Penny rolled over onto her side and reached for his rampant organ, pulling him onto the bed beside her, her hand moving rapidly up and down his shaft. He scrambled over her, manoeuvering himself between her legs but, even as he prepared to thrust into her he felt his penis flagging, growing limp.

Penny looked down and laughed.

'It looks like you might have wasted your money, love,' she said.

He rolled off her, angry with her and himself.

'Do you just want to watch me for a while?' she asked, slipping two fingers into her cleft, gasping exaggeratedly in mock pleasure. Edward sat on the edge of the bed looking first at Penny and then at his own limp organ.

She ceased her movements and lay still.

'Have you ever had a woman before?' she asked, almost scornfully.

He didn't answer.

'You haven't have you?' She laughed, mockingly.

He glanced at her body again, jaws clenched. His body quivering with rage.

'When I said I lived here with my sister,' he began. 'I should have said that she was here tonight. She's in the room just down there.' He motioned in that general direction.

Penny sat up.

'You brought me back here and your fucking sister is in the house?' she said. She was silent for long moments. 'I can get it on with your sister if that's what you want,' Penny offered. 'Is that the reason you brought me back here?'

He nodded.

'I was afraid to ask, in case you refused,' he lied.

Penny smiled.

'As long as the price is right, love . . .' She chuckled and let the sentence trail off, swinging herself off the bed and reaching for her skirt.

'No need to get dressed,' he told her and together they walked, naked, out of the bedroom and along the landing. Edward paused before the door of the last room.

'She's in there,' he said, softly.

Penny listened for any sound of movement from within but there was none.

'Go in,' Edward urged her, watching as she pushed the door open and stepped in.

He reached past her and slapped on the light.

Penny opened her mouth to scream but no sound came forth and she could only clutch both hands to her head in horrified disbelief as she found herself pinned in the blind stare of Maureen's severed head. She turned, moving with surprising speed and her quickness took Edward by surprise. He struck out at her but only succeeded in clipping her shoulder. She dashed past him, shrieking, heading for the stairs, her stomach churning. He snarled and went after her, launching himself at her naked form. He crashed to the ground, swinging both legs round, catching her just above the ankles as she reached the top of the stairs.

Penny screamed again, her arms pinwheeling. She clutched at empty air for long seconds then overbalanced and fell. She struck the stairs hard as she tumbled to the bottom, cracking her head on the wall as she struggled to stop her headlong fall but it was useless. With a final despairing moan, she slumped motionless at the foot of the steps, a vicious gash across her forehead. Edward bounded down after her, grabbing her by the hair, yanking her head up until her face was inches from his own. Blood from the cut was running freely down her face and, when he forced her eyelids apart with two fingers, some of the sticky red fluid found its way between the fleshy flaps. She murmured something and one eye flickered open. Edward was panting madly, his chest heaving. He kept a firm hold on Penny's hair and, unlocking the cellar door, dragged her down into the cold subterranean room. The chill air revived her somewhat but her attempts to push him away were feeble and, as he tugged her the last few feet to the cellar floor, she blacked out.

Thirteen

How long she'd been unconscious Penny couldn't imagine but, as she opened her eyes, she felt her head throbbing where it was cut. She moaned softly and tried to sit up, aware of the cold which seemed to cling to her flesh like a film of freezing dew. She couldn't move her left arm and at first she wondered if she might have broken it in the fall but, as she turned her head, she saw that she had been tied down. Both arms and legs had been strongly secured at ankle and wrist by pieces of nylon string which cut into her flesh every time she tried to wrestle free.

Edward stood at the far end of the work-bench to which Penny was tied, a crazy smile upon his face.

She wanted to ask him what was going on, why she was tied down, what that had been in the bedroom upstairs. Even now her mind would not let her accept that it had been a human head. Her own brain seemed as if it were full of static, a constant and distracting buzz filling it, preventing rational thought.

She saw him walk around the bench, studying her naked body and, through pain-blurred eyes, she saw that he too was still nude. He gently touched the bonds which held her down and stroked her body with his free hand, rubbing her breasts. She saw the grin on his face, his growing erection. Despite the chill in the air, there were beads of perspiration on his face and body. He leant close to her.

'Whore,' he rasped then grinned broadly.

She tried to speak but her mouth was as dry as parchment, her tongue thick and unmoving.

Suddenly he disappeared from her view.

She heard the roar of a powerful engine and it reminded

her of a motorbike, deafening in the silent confines of the cellar.

He lifted the chainsaw into her view, gazing at her over its whirring barbed chain. She tried to scream again but her mouth was clogged with vomit and all she could do was utter a thick liquid gurgle.

Edward was panting for breath. He steadied the McCullough and, with a shout of pleasure, drove the monstrous blade forward. It ripped into her, pulverising the delicate flesh, tearing upwards through her body, the barbs hacking effortlessly onward as he pushed, driving further until they began to churn through her intestines. Blood sprayed in all directions. Now he wrenched it free, briefly hearing the drone of metal on bone as it crunched her pelvis and lower ribs into a thousand splinters. Entrails seemed to snake upwards like the bleeding tentacles of some stricken octopus and a stench so rank it made him sick, wafted up from the riven cavity of her stomach.

Gasping loudly, Edward drew the McCullough across her mutilated torso. Finally, breathless and drenched with blood, he flicked the chainsaw off and stood in the silence looking down at the remains of Penny Dawson's body, his excitement now spent. He held the bloodied chainsaw before him, the muscles in his arms bulging.

He stared at it for long moments then laid it on the floor nearby. He was exhausted but he knew that he must perform his usual ritual. The cleansing after the pleasure. He set about untying the remains of Penny's body and, as he pulled at one of the knots around her ankle he felt something move beneath his hands.

Her left leg came away at the hip and rolled to the floor, landing with a dull thud.

Edward kicked it aside and began unfastening the rest of the ropes.

Fourteen

Todd looked at his watch, muttering to himself when he noticed it had stopped. He looked at the wall clock opposite and re-set his own time piece. It was 1.15 p.m. and he, Vicki and Amy were sitting in a Wimpy Bar drinking coffee. The journalist looked out into the busy street, watching the traffic and hundreds of people as they went about their business.

'Is there something on your mind, Amy?' Vicki asked, looking across at the younger girl.

She shook her head.

'I was wondering when Penny was going to turn up,' said the little Scot. 'I didn't see her yesterday.'

'She probably had a day off' said Vicki, sipping her coffee.

'I thought you lot weren't allowed to do that' said Todd, smiling.

Vicki punched him on the arm.

'What do you mean "you lot"?' she said, 'We have to take a rest every now and then you know.'

'How about a permanent one,' said Todd, looking into her eyes.

'I told you, Dave, I'd think about it,' she said, softly.

'About what?' Amy wanted to know.

Vicki waved a hand before her, dismissing the question.

'Nothing, Amy,' she said.

Todd interrupted her.

'I asked her to give all this up,' he said.

Amy looked surprised.

'Give up the game? What else would you do?' she asked her friend.

Vicki shrugged.

'I don't know but it's tempting,' she said.

Todd reached beneath the table and squeezed her hand, pleased with the warmth of her response.

'What about you, Amy?' he asked. 'Haven't you ever thought of packing it in? Going back to Scotland maybe?'

'Whoring in Glasgow instead of London isn't much of a choice,' she said.

Vicki was the first to see Joe Carter enter the building. He was a powerfully built young man, yet to reach twenty-two but muscular and almost six feet tall. He wore a leather jacket, his long hair flowing over the collar. There were two vicious looking scars on his left cheek and part of the lobe of his left ear was missing, the legacy of a fight he'd had two years before. He had been Penny Dawson's pimp and lover for the past eighteen months. He'd never done a day's work in his life, having lived solely off the money which his tarts brought in.

He spotted the trio sitting in the corner and pushed past a couple of waiters to reach them, swinging himself into the seat beside Amy. Brief 'hellos' were exchanged but the greetings were swift and Carter obviously had something on his mind. He hadn't shaved for a few days and, when he stroked a hand across his chin it made a sound like sandpaper.

'Have any of you seen Penny?' he asked. 'She didn't come home last night.'

Todd and Vicki shook their heads.

'I was with her last night until about eleven,' said Amy. 'She picked up a john, that was the last I saw of her.'

'Bollocks,' rasped Carter.

'It's not like her to be out all night,' said Vicki.

'The guy who she went with,' said Amy. 'He offered to pay her an extra fifty if she stayed the night with him.'

'Fucking hell,' growled Carter. 'She ought to know better than that. What did this geezer look like?'

'He was weird. He hardly spoke but the really peculiar thing was, he gave his name.'

'What was it?' asked the pimp.

'Edward . . . Biggs, something like that. No, Briggs. Edward Briggs. He was driving a white car.'

'And she went off with him?' Carter muttered.

Amy nodded.

'Stupid cow,' he hissed.

'What did this bloke look like?' asked Todd.

'He's about your age. Quite well built,' said Amy.

'Do you know him, Dave?' Vicki asked.

But, instead of an answer, he had got to his feet and dashed out into the street. From inside the snack bar, the others saw the journalist flag down a passing cab and jump into it. No one spoke for long seconds, the silence finally broken by Carter.

'What the hell was all that about?'

It took the taxi less than thirty minutes to reach the offices of *The Herald*. Todd jumped out, payed the driver and dashed in through the main doors. Another five minutes and he was in the records office. There were a couple of other journalists working in there, poring over pieces of micro-film which held information from as far back as the turn of the century. Every issue of the paper was now consigned to a piece of film no bigger than a man's thumbnail. Todd saw what he was looking for and found a vacant display unit. He switched it on and worked the machine, scanning headlines and stories with an unswerving eye.

'Well, if it isn't the prodigal son returned.'

The voice startled him and he turned to see Bill Dougan standing behind him. He was a little man in his early forties, dressed in a faded sports jacket. His face was heavily veined and his nose was purple, attesting to the huge amounts of liquor he consumed. 'Had enough of tits and bums have you?' Dougan asked, chuckling.

'Bill, can you remember a bloke by the name of Edward

Briggs. About my age, maybe a bit older. I'm bloody sure there's something on him in these files. The name rang a bell.'

'I don't know much about *Edward* Briggs,' said Dougan 'But I can remember his father, Ralph. He stabbed his wife to death and then killed himself. I should know, I covered the story myself.'

Todd snapped his fingers.

'I knew I'd heard that name before,' he said. 'What about the son?'

'The son saw it all. He watched his father kill his mother and then commit suicide. I spoke to him not long after it happened. Strange bloke. Still I suppose you couldn't expect him to be a bundle of laughs after what he'd just seen. Why the sudden interest?'

'Well, it seems he's re-surfaced so to speak,' said Todd. 'He picked up a pro last night and no one's seen her since.'

'I wouldn't worry about a missing pro, they come and go like indigestion. Besides, I doubt if his sister would be too happy about him taking "ladies of the night" home with him.' The older man chuckled.

'Sister?' Todd sounded surprised. 'Then he doesn't live alone?'

Dougan held up his hands.

'I don't know if she *still* lives with him,' he said.

Todd nodded.

'Thanks a lot, Bill,' he said.

Dougan turned to leave.

'Have a word with Ron Haggerty,' he said. 'He took the photos. He might have one of Edward and his sister lying about.'

There was a red light on outside Haggerty's dark room when Todd reached it but he knocked nevertheless.

'Hold on,' a gruff voice called from inside and the journalist leant against the wall, studying the notes which he'd made about the case of Ralph and Sheila Briggs, now filed away once more in the maze of micro-film.

After about three minutes, the dark room door opened and Haggerty stuck his head out. A man in his early forties, he sported a thick beard streaked with grey but the top of his head was completely bald as if, somehow, all the hair had decided to take up residence on his chin and cheeks instead of his head. There was a cigarette dangling from his mouth, a long length of ash threatening to drop at any second. He smiled when he saw Todd and the movement did indeed cause the ash to fall.

'I thought you were still working on that Soho thing?' said Haggerty.

'I am,' Todd told him. 'But I need your help, Ron.'

Haggerty motioned for him to enter then closed the dark room door behind them. Todd blinked hard as he stepped inside, trying to adjust to the dull red light inside the room. It was like standing in a room filled with blood.

He repeated his conversation with Bill Dougan. The photographer perched on a stool listening intently. When Todd had finished speaking he nodded and got up, crossing to a bank of filing cabinets one of which he slid open. Todd wrinkled his nose at the smell of developer, peering into a nearby tray where Haggerty was working on some photos of what the reporter assumed were the aftermath of a bank raid. There was one of an overturned security van. Another of the bank itself and a third which showed a man lying on the pavement outside in a pool of dark liquid.

'Edward Briggs and Maureen Briggs,' said Haggerty, handing Todd two photos.

He looked at them carefully, both were dated 22/4/78.

'Any chance of me keeping these for a day or two, Ron?' he asked.

Haggerty nodded and lit up another cigarette. He was about to offer Todd a quick snifter from the bottle of Haig which he always kept in the bottom drawer of the filing cabinet when he saw that the reporter was heading for the door.

'Thanks,' he called and was gone.

Haggerty shrugged his shoulders and decided to have a nip himself.

As Todd sat in the cab on the way back to his hotel he glanced at the two pictures, particularly at the one of Edward. The man was maybe a year or two older than he was but his face was wrinkled, the hard outlines of his chin and forehead making him look more advanced in years than he really was. In the photo, he was standing on the steps outside the house with his sister. She was doing her best to cover her face from the prying eye of the camera but Briggs was looking into it and Todd was sure he could detect the vaguest hint of a smile on the man's lips, as if he were gladly posing for the photo. The reporter sighed heavily and allowed his head to loll back against the rear of the seat. He thought about what Dougan had said;

'Pros come and go like indigestion.'

Maybe Penny Dawson had decided to get up and leave. But, he reasoned, she had no motive for wanting to do so. Joe Carter was her boyfriend, not just her pimp, surely she would not leave without him? Besides, Vicki had told him herself that Penny enjoyed what she did – it didn't make sense for her to leave. Even if she had been seen with Edward Briggs there was still no cause for alarm. It was the man's father who had committed the murder not Edward himself. They weren't even sure if it *was* him who Amy had seen the previous night. She could have misheard the name. She might not identify him in the photo.

Todd rubbed a hand over his face and sat upright again. He was trying to create something out of nothing. He had been sent to Soho by his paper to do a story on vice and now he was trying to solve a missing persons case when the girl in question probably wasn't even missing at all. Penny might not have spent the night with Edward. She could have sneaked out while he was asleep. He shook his head

96

slightly. Then why hadn't she turned up by now? She could be back by the time he returned, he thought.

Todd glanced at his watch. It was nearly 4.05 p.m. The taxi dropped him outside his hotel and he spent the next two hours in his room, typing up some notes and glancing at the photos of Edward and Maureen Briggs.

By seven o'clock, evening was drawing in. Purplish welts of cloud slashed across the darkening sky like badly healed scars.

Another hour and darkness filled the heavens. London began to stir once more as the people of the night took over. Neon glared fiercely, turning the blackness into a kind of artificial twilight. Todd pulled on his leather jacket, stuffed the photos into his pocket and went out.

As he walked up Shaftesbury Avenue, past the theatres, glancing into the windows of restaurants, he wondered if his imagination was working overtime. Perhaps, he told himself, he *wanted* there to be a story here. He dug both his hands deep into his pockets and turned into Dean Street, heading for the area where he knew he would eventually find Vicki and Amy. And probably Penny too.

As it happened he was forced to hang around their patch for thirty minutes before both Vicki and Amy showed up. He saw them both get out of a large foreign car, the younger of the two girls looking down irritably at her black skirt. She held a tissue in one hand and was dabbing at a stain near the waistband. For a moment, Todd remained still, a feeling akin to sadness settling over him as he looked at Vicki, who was running a comb through her ruffled hair, checking her makeup in the mirror she took from her handbag. Then he regained control of himself and crossed to the two girls.

'Hello, Dave,' said Vicki, happily.

He smiled at her, hiding his disappointment expertly enough. Then, reaching inside his pocket he produced the photos.

'Any sign of Penny?' he wanted to know.

'No' Vicki told him, her voice losing its cheerful tone.

The journalist showed the pictures to Amy.

'That's the bloke,' she said without prompting, pointing at Edward Briggs. 'That's him. No mistake.'

Todd nodded and pushed the photos back into his pocket.

'What now?' Vicki asked him. 'Is there anything we can do?'

'Just wait and hope Penny shows up,' he said.

'And if she doesn't?'

He had no answer for her this time.

'I'm going back to the house to change,' said Amy, still dabbing at her skirt. 'If Danny turns up tell him what happened.'

Vicki nodded, watching as her companion left.

'What *did* happen?' asked Todd, a patronising tone to his voice.

Vicki caught the inflection.

'Does it really matter?' she said, irritably.

'Just curious,' he said.

'Sorry, I forgot it was your business to ask questions.' Her voice was heavy with sarcasm.

'What was it? A special for some rich bastard?' he rasped. 'I saw you getting out of the car.'

'Yes, as a matter of fact it was and the reason Amy's going home to change is because the stupid sod shot off all over her skirt. Anything else you'd like to know?'

There was a long silence between them, finally broken by Vicki.

'I'm sorry, Dave,' she said.

He touched her cheek.

'*I'm* sorry,' he echoed. 'I was worried about you that was all.'

They began walking down the street.

'Those photos you showed Amy, was that the reason you dashed off so quick this afternoon?' she wanted to know.

'Yes. I thought the name rang a bell. I was right.' He told her the entire story.

'Oh God,' she murmured.

'I mean, at the moment, there's nothing to link Penny's disappearance with what happened at the Briggs house. I mean, it was five years ago and, besides, Edward Briggs' was never implicated. I just don't like that kind of coincidence.'

'But, if he had a sister, he wouldn't take Penny back to the house surely,' said Vicki.

'No one knows if they still live in the same house now.' He exhaled deeply. 'We're probably worrying for no reason.'

Vicki studied his profile as they walked.

'Do you believe that?' she said.

He didn't answer.

Fifteen

Amy Curtis pulled off her skirt and tossed it onto the bed. Then she crossed to the wardrobe and selected another, a shorter red one with silver stars down both sides. She kept her boots on, standing before the mirror studying her reflection in the glass. She sighed and leaned closer, inspecting the rings beneath her eyes. She decided to apply some fresh make-up before returning to the streets.

She sat down before the dressing table and flipped open her handbag, reaching for her lipstick.

'What the fuck are you doing here?'

The voice startled her and she turned to see Danny Foster standing in the doorway.

'You should be out working,' he barked.

She told him why she was back at the house.

'So, you made fifty tonight,' he said. 'So what? You only made ten last night and fifteen the night before. What the fuck is the matter with you?'

'It's not my fault, Danny,' she said. 'I . . .'

He cut her short.

'I don't want excuses, bitch. Remember who brought you in off the streets. Remember who gave you a fucking home. Me. Well, you better start paying me back otherwise you'll be back where you belong, in the gutter.' He crossed to the dressing table and grabbed Amy by the arm, pulling her to her feet. 'You start earning your keep,' he rasped. 'This isn't a charity.'

She pulled free of him.

'I try my best,' she protested, tears in her eyes.

'Yeah, well I'll see for myself because I'm coming out on the streets with you. I'm going to make sure you bring in a ton tonight, no matter what you have to do to get it.' He threw her coat at her. 'Come on.'

They walked out together, Danny sometimes tugging her along when she slowed down. She wiped a tear from her eye and trudged along beside him until they reached her patch. The pimp exchanged greetings with a number of people as he stood idly in the doorway of a pub sucking on a roll-up.

Amy was the first to see the white Dolomite draw up across the street.

She recognised it immediately and felt her stomach tighten as if her intestines had clotted into a hard knot. She could see the driver sitting motionless behind the wheel and she was sure he was staring at her.

Amy tried to swallow but it was as if someone had put a metal band around her throat and, as she saw the driver of the car get out, she could feel that band tightening.

He was coming towards her.

Edward recognised the girl from the other night and he moved unerringly towards her, seeing the fear flicker across her face. He felt a strange exhilaration as he saw her take a step backwards. For he knew that she was his no matter what. She was there to be taken, just like the other one had been. She *wanted* to be taken, to be used, abused.

'Whore,' he whispered under his breath as he approached.

Danny Foster saw him coming too and he moved closer to Amy.

'Now, you be nice to this man or else I'll break your fucking jaw and you won't work for six months. You'll be out,' he hissed.

'Danny,' she protested. 'He's the one who took Penny Dawson away. He . . .'

The pimp dug her hard in the small of the back.

'I don't know what the fuck you're talking about,' he snarled. 'I just want you to do some work. Got it.'

Edward was upon them by now.

Amy looked into his face and found her gaze met by eyes as cold as chips of ice. He looked first at her then at Foster.

The pimp smiled. His business smile.

'Looking for company, sir,' he said.

Edward nodded, returning his gaze to Amy.

'How much for all night?' he asked and Amy felt something cold run up her spine. She turned and looked at Foster, shaking her head imperceptibly.

'A hundred,' said Foster. 'Now.'

Edward didn't argue. He produced a roll of ten pound notes and pushed the required amount into the outstretched palm of Foster, careful not to touch the pimp's clammy hand. Then he turned and headed back to the car.

'Move it, bitch,' said Foster. 'Don't keep the gentleman waiting.'

Still she hesitated, heart thudding against her ribs.

'I told you what would happen,' Foster snarled and pushed her towards the waiting Dolomite. He stood on the pavement, watching as Amy slid into the passenger seat and Edward, after one more brief look at her, started the engine. The car disappeared into traffic and Foster looked down at the ten pound notes clutched in his hand. He smiled broadly and wandered inside the pub.

The car rapidly left behind the city centre and as they drew further away Amy became more nervous. She looked at Edward but his attention was fixed on the road ahead.

'What's your name?' she asked him, although she knew full well that the answer would only serve to compound her fear.

'Edward Briggs.'

She closed her eyes momentarily. She fought to control her feelings, trying to contain the terror which was building up inside her, winding round her throat like invisible tentacles.

'My name's Amy,' she told him.

He didn't answer.

'You were in that area of London a couple of nights ago weren't you? You picked up a friend of mine.'

Silence.

'Did she meet your sister?'

At last there was a reaction as Edward turned to look at her, taking his eyes of the road and almost swerving into the path of an oncoming van. He glared at her in the gloom of the car, hands gripping the wheel tightly.

'How do you know my sister?' he said, quietly but his voice was full of menace.

'A friend of mine, he remembered your name when he heard it,' said Amy. She swallowed hard. Perhaps he would stop the car and let her out. If he thought that others knew her whereabouts he might just stop and push her out of the vehicle. Drive off and never return. But, he kept his foot firmly on the accelerator and the neon lights of the city centre were soon replaced by the sodium glare of street lamps.

When the car finally came to a halt, Amy had no idea where she was. Edward had pulled into a narrow gravel driveway and she found herself staring through the windscreen at a two storey house which towered menacingly above her as if threatening to topple over. The place was in darkness but no curtains were drawn. She felt that knot in her stomach bunching tighter.

Edward clambered out and she followed him up the short path to the front door which he unlocked, ushering her inside and, immediately, she was struck by the silence which enfolded her like an invisible glove.

'Is your sister at home?' she asked, her voice apparently echoing in the stillness of the hall.

'We won't be disturbed,' said Edward, taking her coat and ushering her towards the sitting room. It smelt musty in there, like something out of a waxworks exhibit, something preserved for all time. Not a thing was out of place and there was a fine film of dust on everything, even the photo of the woman which she noticed propped up on the sideboard. Amy guessed that it must be his sister.

'She's very pretty,' said Amy, pointing at the photo.

Edward swallowed hard.

'Aren't you supposed to ask me what I want?' he said.

'I'm not with you.'

'Your repertoire,' he said, sarcastically. 'How I *want* it.'

Amy shuddered involuntarily.

'How *do* you want it?' she asked.

He smiled thinly but the gesture only served to make her even more uneasy.

'You're different to the other one,' he said. 'At least you appear to be. But I know that all of you are the same deep down. Not just your kind but all women.' He picked up the photo from the sideboard and looked at it. 'I used to think my sister was different but I found out that she was just like all the rest.' He swung those icy eyes onto her again and Amy flinched from them. 'You'll do anything if the price is right, won't you?'

She nodded almost imperceptibly, fearing what he would say next.

He grinned, more broadly this time, his tone lightening.

'A little game,' he chuckled and motioned for her to follow him which she did, out of the sitting room, through the hall to the door which led down into the cellar. He unlocked it and slapped on the lights. Amy shivered as the cold air swirled around her and for a second she hesitated but Edward held out a hand for her to follow him and she did so, eyes scanning the large basement. She saw the work-bench, the wood now dark and stained. The racks of tools, neatly arranged. In one corner there was a metal chair, beside it lay what looked to her like a tool bag.

'I'm a carpenter,' he said, making a sweeping gesture with his arms.

She nodded, heart thumping that little bit faster and, despite the chill in the air, she felt perspiration clinging to her back.

'Get undressed,' he said and it sounded like a command.

She obeyed, divesting herself of her clothes, shivering in the cold. The tiles felt freezing beneath her bare feet and she hugged herself in an effort to keep warm. He stood watching her, one hand behind his back and, as she watched

104

him move towards her, she wondered just what he had picked up.

He swung the mallet with the force of a pile driver, catching her on the jaw, bone snapping loudly under the impact. She felt searing agony for a second and then there was only darkness.

Edward stood over her fallen form, studying the contours of her body for long moments, then he knelt and hooked his hands beneath her armpits, dragging her across the cellar to the metal chair. She was burbling incoherently, the sounds further masked by her inability to form words properly. Part of her broken jaw bone had broken through the skin and Edward found that, as he tied her to the chair, some blood dripped onto his hands.

Satisfied that she was held securely, he hurriedly took off his own clothes and stood before her breathing heavily. She was beginning to come round and the sound which greeted her when she did was a high pitched buzzing, a powerful whirring motor which seemed to grow louder.

If not for her broken jaw she would have screamed. As it was she could only watch, eyes bulging madly in their sockets, as he stood before her grinning wildly.

The power drill vibrated in his grip.

She started to cry, tried to beg him to stop whatever he was going to do but it was useless. She begged for oblivion, praying that the pain in her jaw would cause her to pass out before he reached her but it was not to be.

He stood mere inches away from her, his swollen penis throbbing between his legs, the drill humming loudly on low gear, then he flicked a switch and the pitch intensified as he turned the lethal tool up to full speed. He levelled it, the bit – spinning at over 3500 rpm – aimed at her right eye . . .

Edward switched off the drill and dropped to his knees before Amy's now lifeless remains. He wiped the sweat from his face with one blood-soaked hand, leaving a crimson stain over it. The stench of blood and death was strong in his nostrils but he ignored it. It was something he had grown used to.

'Just like all the rest,' he panted, an all fours now but looking up at the corpse. 'You're all the same. All women. I realized that when Maureen told me she wanted to leave but she was just like mother. They were whores both of them. Except they didn't collect money for their services.' He laughed dryly, a hollow sound without humour. 'The world is better rid of your kind,' he rasped, staring at the corpse. 'Tempters. Is a woman's only function in life to tempt men? To take men's love and throw it in their faces? My mother did that to my father and my sister did it to me. No woman will make a fool of me again.' He got to his feet. 'Your friend, she thought she'd fooled me.' Edward chuckled, the cellar reverberating with that throaty sound – a noise like dry leaves being rustled. 'Your friend is still here. She will always be here. She would have left me, as Maureen would have left me, as my mother would have left my father.'

The anger suddenly seemed to drain from his voice and he smiled again.

'Now you will stay here too,' he said. He chuckled. 'And there will be others.'

Sixteen

Vicki Powell sat on the edge of the bed and took off her shoes, massaging her feet. It was approaching 1.30 a.m. and she was tired but she knew that there were two things which she must do before retiring for the night.

She padded along to the bathroom and took a long shower, soaping herself thoroughly, washing every piece of grime from her body. But as she stood beneath the gushing conduit she realized that the cleansing could only ever be skin deep, running water couldn't wash away the last nine years. Memories and experiences were ingrained within her mind, within her soul, like splinters and, no matter how much she washed, she could never be clean again. She lowered her head, feeling the warm water bouncing against her hair. The rivulets coursed over her shoulders, dripped from her breasts, ran over her stomach and pubic hair. Her belly was very slightly distended, signalling the onset of her period. She was due in another four days and, for the time she was on, she would become a second rate product. There was to be no rest from the job though. That bastard Foster would still have her out on the streets. She could make money other ways than lying on her back he used to say. There were plenty of punters who'd settle for hand jobs. A fiver was better than nothing as far as Danny Foster was concerned. Vicki knew that some of the girls took extra contraceptive pills to prevent themselves coming on but the girl who she had shared the room with prior to Amy had tried the same trick three months running and ended up in hospital with a massive thrombosis.

Amy. Standing beneath the flowing shower outlet, Vicki

wondered where the younger girl was. She hadn't seen her since about nine that evening, since she'd returned to the house to change. Vicki switched off the shower, wiped some water from her face and stood in the silence, thinking. She'd ask Foster when she saw him. She pulled on a bath robe, padded back into her bedroom and took out some money bound with a thick elastic band – her night's takings. She looked at the money then got to her feet and wandered downstairs.

Foster was sitting on the worn sofa, a bottle of Guinness in one hand, a newspaper in the other.

He looked up at Vicki and then returned his attention to the paper.

'Your money,' she said, dropping it onto the table.

'How much?' he asked.

'Aren't you going to count it?'

'I asked you how much.'

'Seventy-five.'

He grinned.

'A good night's work all round,' Foster said. 'That room mate of yours brought me in a ton and there should be more to come when she gets back.'

'Gets back from where?' Vicki wanted to know.

'Some bloke paid a hundred, in advance, if she'd spend the night with him.'

Vicki swallowed hard.

'What did he look like?' she asked, anxiously.

'How the fuck should I know? All punters look alike to me.'

'But you did see him?'

'Yeah, I saw him. He gave me the money himself.'

She described Edward briefly and Foster nodded as she mentioned each detail. 'Was he driving a car?'

'Yeah, a white Dolomite, why?' he wanted to know.

But already Vicki was on her feet, dashing out of the room.

Foster opened his mouth to say something but decided not to bother. He took a swig from his bottle and set about counting the money which she had dropped before him.

Vicki dressed quickly, pulling on a pair of black cords and a dark sweatshirt. Her hair was still damp in places but it didn't worry her. She had more important things on her mind. She stepped into a pair of ankle boots and fastened her coat then she hurried down the stairs once more, not even pausing when Foster shouted to ask her where she was going. He ran to the door and looked out but she had already disappeared into the darkness, further camouflaged by her clothing.

'You stay away from that fucking reporter,' the pimp shouted after her.

Seventeen

If there *was* a desk clerk on duty in the reception of the Venus Hotel, he certainly wasn't in evidence when Vicki slipped through the doors into the reception. She glanced furtively around and heard some sounds coming from a small room behind the desk. She could hear a kettle beginning to whistle and, for fleeting seconds, she caught sight of someone through the half open door. As quietly as she could she crossed to the desk and glanced at a large ledger which passed as the register. Vicki scanned it, looking up periodically for any signs of movement from the room behind the desk. She could hear the chink of metal on china as the man stirred his tea. Then, she saw it.

D. Todd . . . . . Room 17

Ahead of her was the lift, to her right the double doors which led to the dining room. But, slightly to the left of the lift was another door which she guessed would lead to the stairs.

Her assumption was right and she peered over her shoulder to see a burly man with an ill-fitting suit emerge from the room beyond the desk carrying a cup of steaming fluid. Vicki smiled to herself and set off up the stairs, moving quickly but quietly until she came to the first floor. It took her a matter of minutes to find number seventeen and she knocked gently, eyes scanning the narrow corridor for fear of waking any of the other guests.

There was no answer.

Muttering under her breath she knocked again, a little harder.

There were sounds of movement from inside and she heard a key being turned in the lock. A moment later the door opened and a slightly bewildered Todd blinked out at her.

'Vicki,' he said. 'What's wrong? It's . . .' He looked at his wrist, realizing that he didn't have his watch on.

She pushed past him and shut the door. Todd sat down on the edge of the bed, just a sheet across his groin. He ran a hand through his hair and yawned.

Vicki looked around the room. It was small, less than fifteen feet square. Dark brown wallpaper covered the plaster which was showing through in places. The carpet was threadbare beside the bed itself. There was a small washbasin next to the window. Todd had set up his typewriter on the old sideboard, a piece of paper hung from the roller. A bell saying 'Ring for Maid' had been plastered over with electrical tape.

'What's wrong?' Todd asked, his head clearing a little.

'It's Amy,' Vicki began. 'She went off with Edward Briggs tonight.'

'Oh Christ, how do you know?'

'Foster told me.'

'But he doesn't know what Briggs looks like.'

'I described him, the description matched. Foster told me what sort of car Briggs was driving.' She swallowed hard. 'There couldn't have been any mistake. It *was* him. He paid a hundred quid and asked if Amy could stay the night.'

The journalist scratched his head as if trying to force some coherent thought into his head.

'What the hell are we going to do, Dave?' she asked, imploringly.

'Well, I don't think we can go to the police,' he muttered. 'We don't even know if anything *has* happened to Penny or Amy.'

'You were the one who was suspicious,' she rasped and he waved a hand for her to keep her voice down.

'Look,' he began. 'We can't go to the police, right? That means we'll have to trace the two girls ourselves. That's not going to be easy.'

'You know where he lives.'

'What exactly do you think he's done to them, Vicki?'

'I don't know but I intend to find out.' She looked at him. 'With or without your help.'

'I'll help you,' he said. 'But we can't go to Briggs' house, we can't accuse him of anything and we certainly can't break in and search the place. We know that Penny and Amy were both seen with him but that's all we know.'

'We also know that they're both missing.'

There was a long silence.

'What about his sister?' said Vicki.

'We don't even know if she's still living with him,' Todd protested.

'If we could contact her, she might be able to tell us what Edward's up to.'

'I doubt it. If he's taking girls home then he's either living on his own or *he's* moved out. Maybe he had sex with them in the car.'

'So,' she said, challengingly. 'What are we going to do?'

'I know a couple of people at Scotland Yard . . .'

She cut him short.

'You said we couldn't involve the police.'

'They're friends,' he assured her. 'They've given me information before. Off the record. They might know something. It's worth a try.'

Vicki exhaled deeply and sat down on the chair by the sideboard. Todd looked at her for long seconds, thinking how vulnerable she looked. She smelt of soap, a delicate scent which complemented rather than covered the smell of her own body oils.

'Does Foster know you're here?' asked the journalist.

'I should think he's got a pretty good idea,' she said.

'Why did you come to *me*, Vicki?' he asked, hoping for the answer he was formulating in his mind.

'I knew you were the only one I could trust,' she said, looking at him across that grubby little room. 'You were the only one who would care.'

He smiled.

'And, I wanted to be with you,' she added, getting to her feet. She crossed to the bed and slipped her hand tentatively into his. They sat like two teenagers holding hands for the first time. He touched her chin, turning her head so that she was looking at him and he saw her eyes misting over. A single tear formed in the corner of her eye and trickled down her cheek. Todd wiped it away with his index finger then slowly leant forward. Their mouths locked and, for long seconds, they remained joined, tongues moving feverishly, each in the warmth and moistness of the other's mouth.

'And now you're with me?' he asked softly.

'I want to stay,' she said.

Todd felt one expert hand slide onto his thigh, working higher to envelop his testicles and then his penis which grew rigid under her careful teasing. She pulled the sheet away to reveal his bulging manhood, dropping to her knees to kiss the bulbous head. Todd gasped and stroked her thick hair, enduring the delicious attentions of her tongue for a couple of minutes then he urged her to join him, lifting her face and kissing her on the forehead.

She deftly pulled off her boots and joined him on the bed. Vicki was about to remove her cords when she realized that there was no rush. This was not a customer she was with, it was a man she felt very strong feelings for.

Todd slid one hand inside her sweatshirt, allowing it to trace a path over her skin until he reached one taut breast, the nipple already swollen and hard. He took it between his thumb and forefinger and squeezed gently, feeling her body quiver as he began to knead first one breast then the other. With his help she removed the sweatshirt and dropped it beside the bed. For her own part, she closed her hand around his shaft, twisting slightly to allow him access to her zip which he undid. She lay on her back and kicked off her cords and the two of them lay naked across the bed.

Todd could not control his impatience and he slid over her, guided into her burning cleft by her willing hands. He took the weight on his elbows and thrust into her. As he did so, she raised her legs, locking her ankles around the small of his back as he plunged into her, coaxing each firm stroke, rotating her hips until Todd realized that he was losing control. He slowed his own pace but Vicki kept on moving beneath him, despite his protests. They kissed again and Todd's hands gripped the sheet as his muscles tightened and he felt the waves of pleasure flowing over him.

He withdrew from her almost reluctantly, breathing heavily. She kissed him softly on the lips then the two of them lay side by side once more.

'I'm sorry, Vicki,' he said, apologising for his loss of control.

'There's no need to be sorry, Dave,' she said, pulling the sheets up and drawing closer to his hot body.

They lay in the darkened room without speaking for what seemed like an eternity then Todd turned his head and looked at her.

'You go to work when you get in bed don't you?' he asked.

'What do you mean?' Vicki wanted to know.

'With every man. This is just a bit of overtime.'

'That's not true, Dave. Not with you.'

'Then why couldn't you . . .' He let the sentence trail off.

'You think it's your fault because I didn't come, is that it?' she said.

He nodded.

'Never in my life have I had sex with a man who saw me as anything else but something to be used. I might as well be a blow up doll to most of the johns. After a while you start to believe it about yourself. You feel that you're there for *their* pleasure. As long as *they're* satisfied that's all that matters.' She paused. 'I don't enjoy what I do, Dave and I try to make damn sure I never start enjoying it.' She kissed him on the cheek. 'Give me time that's all I ask. Time to learn what it's like to be with someone who wants to *give* pleasure too.'

'But how can you, living the life you do?' he said.

'Well, perhaps I won't be living that sort of life much longer.'

He raised his eyebrows.

'You thought about what I said? About giving up the game?'

'Yes. I thought about it. I know you're right. I want to get out, get away from it but it's not that easy, Dave.'

He hugged her closer to him.

'We'll find a way.' There was reassurance in his voice. 'And I can give you as much time as you need.'

'What about you?' she enquired. 'There must have been other girls. How come you're not married by now?'

'Married?' he exhaled deeply. 'I don't think I've ever thought about it.' His voice took on a reflective tone. 'Although there was one girl, three or four years ago. We lived together for a while.'

'What happened?'

'She wanted to get married. I didn't see anything wrong with the way things were. I couldn't understand how a ring was going to make our way of life any better or worse. Besides, I didn't want to make a commitment.'

'Didn't you love her?'

'Yes, I loved her. As much as I was capable of loving anyone but she could never understand that my career meant more to me than everything else. She wasn't prepared to take a back seat to my ambitions. She packed her bags one night and walked out. She left a note pinned to the typewriter.' He smiled, sardonically. 'I suppose she realized that would be the one place I'd be sure to find it.'

'So you live on your own now?'

He nodded.

'I've got a place in Holborn. Just a flat but it's big enough.' He smiled at her, running one hand through her thick brown hair.

'I wouldn't want to go through life alone. Not all of my life,' she said softly.

'I don't plan on spending *all* of my life alone,' he intoned.

'You had someone though. You had someone who loved *you*. That's what really matters. Knowing that someone cares for you. I'd just like, once, to know what that feels like.' She laid her head on his chest, listening to the steady thumping of his heart.

Now, more than ever before since he'd met her, Todd felt that curious mixture of affection and pity for Vicki. He placed his hand on the back of her neck and stroked the soft flesh.

It gets to the stage where you lose your feelings,' she said. 'You lose your emotions and when someone comes along who you *do* care about it's frightening. I'm frightened now, Dave. Frightened to let go. I don't want to get hurt, I don't want you to be the one who hurts me.'

'I won't,' he promised her. 'I . . .' The words trailed off once again.

I love you? Is that what you were going to say, he asked himself. After so short a time could he even have begun to love Vicki? He knew that it was unlikely and yet there was something there, gnawing away inside him – an affection which was much stronger than it should have been. He closed his eyes, her soft hair caressing his chest as she moved her head.

She held him tight and drifted off to sleep, feeling more secure than she'd felt for many years.

Eighteen

Edward Briggs crossed to the bedroom window and looked out into the street. All but one of the street lamps were off and the car which drew up a little way down the road was visible only by the glare of its headlamps which cut through the impenetrable gloom like laser beams.

Edward saw the car discharge three or four people but, with the sound-proofing in the house, he could hear nothing. It was like watching a scene from a silent film. He pulled his dressing gown tight around him and padded across to the door, the only sound was that of the clock beside his bed. It's hands glowed green in the darkness showing the time to be just after two a.m.

He closed the door behind him and wandered across to the last door on the landing. The key was in the lock and it made a loud clicking sound as he turned it. A putrid odour escaped from the room and Edward coughed as it swirled around him in a reeking cloud. He moved over to the bed and stood beside it, looking down at the severed head of Maureen.

It was in an advanced state of putrefaction now. The skin had lost that waxy sheen and was now dull and flabby. The eyelids were closed, covering the eyes which were now almost fluid – soft mushy balls which looked like coagulating grease. One ear had withered like a flower exposed to flame and the eyebrows and lashes had come away in places. A clear fluid had trickled from both nostrils and solidified on the drooping top lip. The cheeks were sunken, a piece of bone showing through on the left side.

He gazed at the rotting head for long moments, trying to ignore the rank odour which it gave off, conscious of the fact that the same smell had begun to permeate the entire house.

He lingered a moment longer beside the decaying object then turned and headed for the stairs.

He felt more secure in the darkness and the house seemed to close in around him as he wandered its dark rooms and narrow corridors. Sleep had eluded him these past two nights and he had taken to walking about in the small hours, enjoying the seclusion. Even though the lengthy rituals of cleaning up usually exhausted him he had still found it difficult to sleep. He had thought about taking one of the pills which Maureen used to take. They were in a suitcase with the rest of her clothes. But he had decided against that. Now he stood before the door to what had been the dining room, the key in his hand and he noticed that the smell was almost overpowering. It hit him like a palpable blast as he opened the door. But he reined back his revulsion and stepped inside.

It always seemed quieter than ever in this particular room and Edward pulled up one of the antique chairs and sat down, looking around him in the gloom. The curtains were kept drawn, even during the daylight hours, despite the fact that the room was at the back of the house. As with all the others, it had adjoining doors linking it to the kitchen on one side and the hallway on the other.

As if he were in some hallowed temple, Edward bowed his head and closed his eyes. Thoughts tumbled through his mind. Of Maureen. Of his parents. Of the girls he had brought to the house and, a slight smile formed across his face as he remembered them, held helpless before him. *He* was the stronger one. This was *his* house now. He opened his eyes and looked around again, getting to his feet.

If only Maureen hadn't tried to leave him. If she hadn't betrayed him things might have been different. She had tried to leave him, condemn him to a life of solitude. Alone in *his* house. But he wasn't alone. Maureen was still with him.

And there were others too.
There would be more.
He made his way up the stairs.

Nineteen

'All right, bitch, where's the money?'

Danny Foster was still sitting on the worn old sofa, his shirt open to the waist, the empty Guinness bottle on the cushion beside him.

Vicki took off her coat, eyeing the pimp warily. She had left the Venus Hotel before dawn and walked the short distance from there to Earlham street, not expecting to find Foster waiting for her when she returned. Now she swallowed hard and looked at the thick set form slumped before her. There was a wicked, challenging gleam in his eye and he was tapping slowly on the empty bottle, his uneven nails making a persistent chinking sound.

'What money?' asked Vicki.

'The money from the trick. You went out last night to meet a john, didn't you?' He smiled, his lips curling upward into a sneer.

'There isn't any money, Danny,' she told him.

'Oh. You felt sorry for him so you let him have it for nothing, eh? You decided it was time for a few freebies?'

'I'm telling you, there's no money.'

'Well, if you were with a customer there must be,' he snarled. 'Unless of course you were with that fucking reporter.'

'Look, just forget about it, Danny, I'll make up the cash today. Right?' She headed for the stairs but Foster leapt to his feet and grabbed her arm, breathing rancid, beer-soaked fumes into her face.

'Forget about it, nothing,' he rasped. 'I told you to keep away from that cunt. He's been nosing around here for too long as it is. How many times have I got to tell you?'

She never even saw the blow coming.

Foster struck her hard across the face with the back of his hand and she went reeling. As she tried to straighten up he grabbed her by the hair and pulled her to her feet.

'I own you, bitch,' he growled and punched her, the impact making her see stars. For long moments bright light flashed before her eyes and her head spun.

The pimp dragged her to her feet once more, his eyes blazing with anger.

'You ever try ro run out on me and I'll cut your tits off. Got it?'

She didn't answer.

'Got it?' he bellowed into her face and struck her again. She fell onto the sofa, blood trickling from the rent in her lip. One eye was half closed and she could already feel it beginning to swell up. It was watering, throbbing as if someone were trying to push it out of her head from the inside.

She looked at Foster.

'You bastard,' she murmured. 'One day someone's going to break your neck.'

The pimp grinned.

'Well it won't be you will it, bitch, eh?'

Vicki touched her lip tentatively and felt the cut, saw blood on her finger tips.

'Damaging your merchandise isn't very clever, Danny,' she said, dabbing at the cut with a handkerchief. 'Punters aren't going to look at a girl who looks as if she's just been three rounds with Henry Cooper.'

'Well you'd better hope they do, otherwise, like I told you, you'll be out in the gutter again.' He paused for a moment. 'And where the hell is that room mate of yours? The bitch isn't back yet. If she's done a runner I'll . . .'

Vicki cut him short.

'Amy's still out?' she said anxiously.

'Yeah. She was supposed to be spending all night with the bloke but she should have been back by now.'

'You mean with Edward Briggs?'

'I don't know what his fucking name was. All I know is she should be bringing back a nice little hand out and I want to know where she is.'

Vicki swallowed hard and got to her feet, a little unsteadily at first.

'I'm going up to my room,' she said.

'Put some ice on that eye,' Foster told her. 'It'll take the swelling down.'

'Why the sudden interest?' she said.

'I'm safeguarding my investment,' he told her, grinning.

'Then maybe you should be worrying about Amy.'

'She'll be back. She knows where she's well off. Besides, she's got nowhere else to go.'

Vicki headed for the stairs.

'You can't stop me seeing him, Danny,' she said.

'If you mean that reporter, forget it. I told you what would happen if you did.' He reached into his back pocket and pulled something out. Vicki froze as she heard the swish, click of a flick knife. The pimp held it before him, the vicious point aimed at her chest. 'I'll cut you up so bad you'll look like a fucking jig-saw.' He paused. 'And him too.'

Vicki turned her back and made her way slowly up the stairs to the bedroom she shared with Amy. The other girl's bed had not been slept in, her discarded clothes still lay where they'd been left the previous night. Vicki crossed to the mirror and looked at her own face, inspecting the cuts and the dull purplish bruise that had begun to form around her right eye.

'Bastard,' she muttered as she touched the bruise, wincing as she did so. Through the mirror she could see Amy's bed. She thought about Briggs. Of how Penny Dawson had still not turned up. First her and now Amy. Vicki shuddered involuntarily and wondered who was going to be the next one to run into Edward Briggs.

Outside, the sun was forcing its way from behind a bank of early morning mist.

It was 9.36 a.m.

Twenty

The chisel seemed to waver in his grip for a second as he steadied the mallet but then, using all his strength, Edward struck the plastic handle of the lethal tool. It went several inches into its appointed mark and he smiled, putting some weight on it.

There was a loud tearing sound, much like splintering bone, as the cupboard door came loose, its rusty hinges falling at his feet. He pulled the door away and laid it on the sheets of newspaper provided.

'The last people who lived here put the cupboards in,' Helen Patterson told him, watching as he set to work with the chisel again, hacking what remained of the rotting cupboards free of their place beneath her sink. Helen was a tall woman in her late twenties, dressed in a baggy sweater and faded drainpipe jeans. She could easily have passed for a teenager. Only her face, rounded and mature, showed the passage of years. There was a frightful noise from the next room and she turned hurriedly to see what was going on.

Edward watched her departure, running appreciative eyes over her perfectly curved buttocks, accentuated by the denim which hugged them so tightly. Then he returned to the job in hand, selecting a larger chisel from the row of tools which he had laid out on a piece of dirty linen, within easy reach when he needed them.

'All right,' he heard her shout from the next room. 'Who did this?'

Silence.

'Keith, was it you? Tracy?'

Still no answer.

'Well you'd better behave or I'll take your toys away.'

Helen returned, muttering to herself.

'Kids,' she said smiling. 'Have you got any?'

Edward shook his head.

'I'm not married,' he said.

Helen chuckled.

'That doesn't mean anything these days. You could still have . . .'

He cut her short, the contempt open and blazing in his eyes.

'I said I wasn't married.'

Helen raised her eyebrows and peered at the back of his head. She felt curiously uneasy about this man and had done ever since he arrived. However people had told her what a good worker he was and he had agreed to do the jobs she asked for what, she considered, was a very reasonable price. It was his manner she didn't like. He was cold, distant. Even a little frightening.

Edward watched her as she laid the kitchen table for lunch and he glanced at his watch, noting that it was almost noon.

'Your dinner will be ready soon,' she called. 'What do you want with your fish fingers?'

Two tiny voices shouted unanimously.

'Chips.'

Helen smiled and crossed to the larder. She muttered under her breath. No potatoes. She would have to nip down to the shop to get some. She looked hard at Edward, hacking away with the chisel and coughed lightly.

'Excuse me,' she began. 'But would you mind keeping an eye on the kids while I go to the shop? I won't be five minutes.'

He nodded.

Helen passed through into the living room and Edward heard her telling the two children where she was going. A second later the front door slammed behind her. Immediately, two inquisitive faces appeared at the kitchen door.

Keith, a year older than his sister at six, walked into the room and sat down cross-legged near Edward who glanced disdainfully at the boy.

'What are you doing?' the lad asked, watching as Edward hacked the remainder of the door away with a chisel.

'Working,' he replied, sharply.

It was Tracy's turn to join in. She picked up a small tenon saw which Edward hurriedly snatched away from her.

'Leave the tools alone,' he said.

But the kids were fascinated by the array of hardware set out before them and Keith could not resist touching one of the long screwdrivers. He sniffed his fingers and they smelt like rusty metal. Tracy did the same and both the children giggled. Edward continued working, trying to ignore them but finding it increasingly difficult. He got to his feet and plugged in his powersaw, hefting it in his hand before switching it on. The six inch blade, moving up and down at more than 2,500 strokes per minute, cut effortlessly through the wood and sent a spray of fine dust into the air.

The two kids had now turned their attention to Edward's butane blow torch and he swiftly turned off the powersaw when he saw Keith pick it up.

'Leave the things alone,' he rasped through clenched teeth.

'What does that do?' the little boy asked, pointing at the blow torch.

'It burns,' Edward told him. 'It'll burn you if you don't leave it alone.'

He returned to his cutting, the kids asking question after question until he was sick of hearing their voices. They seemed to reverberate in his mind, mingling with the sound of the saw.

The saw.

God, how easy it would be to turn it on them. To hack through those tiny limbs. He gritted his teeth and tried to ignore them.

Tracy touched the blade of the utility knife, not realizing its razor sharpness until it sliced open her finger tip. She stared at the dripping cut for a second then her face darkened and she began to cry. Loud sobs which racked her tiny body. Sobs which seemed to pound in Edward's ears, inside his brain. Louder even than the whirring of the saw. He switched it up to its full speed, up to 3,000 strokes per minute.

Still she cried. Louder it seemed.

'Shut up,' he murmured under his breath.

A bead of perspiration burst onto his forehead.

Shut up.

Tracy continued to cry, holding the cut finger before her.

SHUT UP.

Edward could stand it no longer. That persistent wailing. He turned towards her, the saw humming in his grip, anger etched across his face.

SHUT UP.

It would be so easy to shut her up. Two or three quick thrusts with the saw. First the girl, then the boy.

He smiled thinly and looked into her eyes, the saw buzzing madly, his own breath coming in gasps.

He was less than a foot away from them.

The back door opened and Helen walked in, clutching a bag of potatoes. She tripped over the lead of the Jigsaw. Edward shot her a wary glance.

'Sorry, Mr Briggs,' she said. 'I nearly pulled the plug out.'

He switched the power tool off and, in the new found peace, Helen saw and heard her daughter crying.

'What have you done?' she said, embracing the little child. She noticed the cut on Tracy's finger and sucked at it, wrapping a handkerchief around the wounded digit.

'She did it on one of that man's knives,' said Keith, still looking at the saw.

Helen tutted.

'You silly girl, that'll teach you not to touch things that don't belong to you.'

Edward watched as Helen lifted her daughter up and carried her into the sitting room, followed by Keith.

He wiped the perspiration from his face, his eyes locked on the power saw, his breathing rapid. He closed his eyes for a second then, heart pounding, he lifted the saw once again and returned to his work.

Twenty-one

The last dart sank into the yellow of the treble band and Peter Fraser smiled, smugly. Todd chalked up the score, took a sip of his vodka then took his place before the board.

'So, what do you want to know?' Fraser asked.

He had to raise his voice to make himself heard, the public bar of The Bell being full, the time at 1.15 p.m. The policeman's voice was deep, thick bass, but it carried over the din with an authority which matched his appearance. He was nearly six foot five, about four years older than Todd. He had been on the force for more than fifteen years, the last six of those as a sergeant. Hands like ham hocks hung by his side and, when he lifted his pint glass, it was like a giant holding a thimble. He wore an open neck shirt and a dark blue blazer which was tight across the shoulders. A pair of jeans, still new and stiff, completed his attire.

'Now what makes you think I want something, Pete?' said Todd, finishing on double top and returning to the table.

'Because every time it's my day off and you offer to buy me a drink, you want something.'

Todd smiled.

'You've got a suspicious mind, Pete.'

'No I haven't. It's just that I've known you too long for you to be able to fool me any more.'

Both men laughed.

Todd held up his hands.

'All right, I admit it, I do need your help.' He looked at the policeman through a fog of smoke which was rising from the cigarette butt he'd just ground out. '*Off* the record.'

'That's what I figured,' said Fraser.

'Do you remember, about five years ago, a bloke called Ralph Briggs killed his wife and then committed suicide? It happened in a house in Kilburn.'

Fraser nodded.

'There were two kids,' Todd continued. 'Well, not kids when it happened but you know what I mean. The son, Edward, was a bit older than me. But there was a daughter too. They both still live in the house.'

'So?'

'Well its probably got nothing to do with it but two . . . friends of mine, young women, have gone missing lately and both of them were seen with Edward Briggs.'

'And you think he's got them?'

'It's possible.'

'Like father, like son eh?' said Fraser, chuckling.

'I just wondered if you'd heard anything.'

'Well, if two girls had been kidnapped or murdered then I might have heard something. As it is, I've heard nothing.'

'Does that mean you have heard but *can't* tell me or you've heard but *won't* tell me?' Todd asked.

'Now who's being suspicious?' Fraser said, smiling.

'I said off the record, Pete, for Christ's sake.'

'I'm not pissing you about, Dave, I've heard nothing about two young women going missing in the past two days.'

Todd looked disappointed.

'I have heard something about Edward Briggs' sister though,' the policeman continued and the journalist sat up, suddenly attentive.

'Does she still live with him?' he asked.

'She *did*. About a month ago he filed a missing persons report on her. He reckoned she'd run off with a boyfriend or something. The constable who took his statement said the poor sod was really upset about it.'

'So he's been in that house on his own for more than a month?'

'It looks that way. So what if he has?'

'Any news of the sister?' Todd wanted to know.

'Not a trace so far. Not of her or the boyfriend.' The policeman regarded his friend impassively and it was he who finally broke the silence. 'What is on your mind, Dave?'

Todd lit up another cigarette.

'Three women have disappeared in the last month, each one somehow connected with Edward Briggs.'

'But you can't say that for sure. What about these two friends of yours. They weren't connnected with him in any way.'

'He was the last one they were seen with.'

'That's no reasonn to suspect him of kidnapping or murder. It's just coincidence.'

Todd snorted.

'Three girls in a month. Do me a favour, Pete.'

1 'You've got an over-active imagination, that's your trouble.'

'Maybe, but I still think it's bloody strange.' The journalist took a piece of paper from his pocket and scribbled two phone numbers on it. He pushed it across the table to Fraser. 'If you hear anything, Pete, call me will you?' He got to his feet.

Fraser nodded but, as the reporter turned to leave, Fraser called him back.

'Dave,' he said, wagging a finger reproachfully. 'If this little story turns out to be right, you let us handle it. We can do without any heroics.'

Todd winked at him and was gone, leaving the policeman to gaze at the phone numbers. He finished his pint then went and got another.

'Shit,' grunted Todd, hitting the wrong key for the third consecutive time. He backspaced and erased his mistake succeeding in typing the word at the fourth attempt, then he pulled the paper from the roller and scanned what he had written. It was the final part of his assignment and he knew, instinctively, that it wasn't right. He wasn't saying what he wanted to say. He got to his feet and crossed to the wash basin, picking up the plastic beaker on the side. The tap spluttered for a second then Todd filled the beaker with cold water and drank. He looked across at the typewriter. It was no good, his mind wasn't on his work, it was on the disappearance of the three women. It was on Edward Briggs. It was on Vicki. In fact, it was anywhere but on his work. Todd drained what was left in the beaker and refilled it, returning to his seat.

There had to be a link between Briggs and the missing women. Why had all three disappeared without trace? Fraser had said that it could just be coincidence and, for fleeting seconds, Todd might have agreed. But not now. He was certain. He *wanted* there to be a link. There was quite a story in this somewhere and *he* wanted to be the one to uncover it. With Vicki's help he would.

Vicki.

An image of her flashed into his mind and refused to leave. Todd was under no illusions now about his true feelings for her. When this assignment was over he would leave here and return to his flat in Holborn and he would take her with him. He was sure she would come. He sipped at his water, feeling almost guilty about the way he felt for her. Even now she could be in that house in Earlham street with another man. 'Working.' But the thought angered rather than revolted him and it angered him because she was forced to do that kind of thing to earn money. Angry also that men like Danny Foster used girls to keep themselves in comfort. And Todd had some anger reserved for himself. For, in a way, he too intended using Vicki.

Briggs had shown a liking for prostitutes. Eventually, he would be back in the area.

Even as he sat at the typewriter, the reporter was formulating a plan to trap Briggs.

But, for it to be successful, he would need to use Vicki.

Twenty-two

Night seemed to draw in more rapidly than usual and it brought with it a harsh wind which Todd found bit at his lips and the end of his nose as he walked. He pulled up the collar of his jacket and dug both hands deep into his pockets. All around him the familiar roar of traffic filled the air, petrol fumes and diesel mingling with the odour of cooking meat which wafted from the numerous take-aways which he passed. In one, an enormous joint of lamb was turning slowly on a rotisserie while a fat Greek dressed in a striped overall carved from it, dispensing the dripping portions to those who waited.

At the corner of Shaftsbury Avenue and Frith Street, a car had broken down and the journalist glanced across as the unfortunate driver fumbled about beneath the bonnet while cars behind him blasted their hooters and attempted to squeeze by the stricken vehicle. No one attempted to help the driver.

Todd continued up the street, past the usual array of strip clubs, massage parlours and cinemas which he had come to know so well. He even nodded greetings to one or two of the people who stood in the doorways of clubs and pubs. A young girl whom he had seen many times in the past fortnight waved happily to him from across the street and Todd waved back. He knew the kid was barely sixteen. She had, he'd been informed, been on the streets since she was thirteen. He slowed his pace for a moment, watching her as she walked away, arm linked with a tall man who must have been well into his forties.

Todd shook his head and walked on. That was the way things were around Soho. There came a time when nothing caused a ripple of emotion any longer because the place was devoid of it. There was sex in abundance, in magazines, in person, to buy and sell. But nowhere in this stinking hole was there any emotion. No one could afford the luxury.

Todd reached the patch which he knew Vicki worked and glanced around the procession of sanguine faces which passed him, looking for her. He sucked in an anxious breath. Perhaps she was with a bloody customer. Or with Edward Briggs.

He forced the thought from his mind and wandered across to the café on the corner of the street. The girls sat in the window drinking cups of luke-warm coffee and he recognised one of them. She was a coloured girl, known on the streets as Roxanne though her real name was Shirley. Todd knew that she shared the same house as Vicki. They were, as the pimps liked to put it, both in the same stable.

The journalist walked into the cafe, unzipping his jacket as he did so surprised at the intensity of the heat inside. He walked across to the table and both girls looked up in surprise.

'Have either of you seen Vicki Powell?' he asked.

'Why?' asked Shirley.

'I just want to know if you've seen her.'

The black girl shrugged.

'Well, have you or not?' Todd rasped, irritably, his voice attracting the attention of the other customers in the place. They looked round to watch the little tableau before them.

Shirley put down her coffee cup.

'She's probably got business.'

'You live in the same place as her, have you seen her?'

The coloured girl looked at him, her voice low when she spoke.

'Look, man. Danny told all of us to keep away from you. Now I don't want my face cut so why don't you just leave me alone.'

'I don't give a fuck what that slimy little bastard told you,' he growled. 'Have you seen Vicki or not?'

'She's working this patch as usual, she's somewhere

around, I saw her ten or fifteen minutes ago,' Shirley told him. 'Satisfied?'

'Thanks for your help,' said Todd, sarcastically and stalked out.

The wind immediately bit into him again, a marked contrast to the stifling heat inside the cafe. He walked the streets slowly, eyes alert, searching the bustling crowds for her.

It was another ten minutes before he spotted her. She was standing in a doorway talking to a man and Todd almost let out an audible sigh of relief when he laid eyes on her. At least Edward Briggs had not picked her up. She was dressed in a pair of black satin trousers which cut into her figure at strategic places, outlining every curve and bulge. Long white boots were pulled up over her knees and she had a white blouse on and, even from a distance, he could see the dark outline of her nipples through the thin material.

Todd stood watching as Vicki spoke to the man who was continuously looking her up and down. However, after a moment or two he shook his head and walked off. She reached into her handbag and took out a cigarette, lighting one up. The journalist took his cue and scuttled across to her.

Vicki saw him coming and lowered her head, not even raising it when she greeted him. He frowned.

'I've been looking for you,' he said.

'And now you've found me,' she said and he detected a hint of detachment in her voice. She continued looking down at the ground, grinding a spent match beneath the toe of her boot.

'What's wrong, Vicki?' he asked, touching her cheek, surprised when she pulled away.

'I don't feel too well, Dave,' she lied. 'That's all it is.'

He noticed how she was keeping her face away from him and, without warning he grabbed her chin and pulled her around so that he was gazing into her eyes. But it was not her eyes he was studying. He saw the cut on her lip, hidden to a certain degree by lipstick but the swelling and colour of the bruise around her right eye could not be disguised even though she had tried by using foundation cream and powder. There were scratches too on her cheek.

'Who did this to you?' he hissed through clenched teeth.

'Dave . . .'

He grabbed her by the shoulders.

'Who did this?' he snarled. 'Some fucking freak?'

She shook her head.

'No,' he said, his breath coming in gasps. 'It was that bastard Foster wasn't it?'

She didn't answer.

'Wasn't it?' he rasped.

'Dave, don't get involved,' she said. 'He told me what would happen if I kept on seeing you. *I* knew what would happen. It's not your business.'

'It is now.'

He glared at her.

'I know that house is in Earlham street. Now, *you* either tell me where it is or I'll find out from someone else but I want a word or two with that shitbag.' His voice was thick with anger.

She nodded.

'I'll show you,' Vicki said and together they set off along the street. Todd hardly spoke, his face set in hard lines.

'When did he do it?' the reporter wanted to know.

'This morning,' Vicki confessed, having to almost run to keep up with him. 'When I got back. He knew I'd been with you.'

Todd didn't speak.

They crossed the street, the journalist almost running, as if anxious to reach the house. When they finally did, he paused outside, looking up at the grime-encrusted brickwork. It was a three storey building, identical to many others around it. He reached out to bang the knocker but Vicki pulled his hand away, producing a key from her purse. She opened the door and they walked in, Todd recoiling from the smell of damp in the hallway. There was a waste bin there, filled with old newspapers and topped

135

with an empty whisky bottle. Ahead of him were the stairs, to his left the door which led into the sitting room. As he walked across to it he could hear sounds coming from inside. He looked at Vicki who also heard the noises and pressed her ear close to the door. There were voices. Soft, hushed voices which did not form words and, as Todd pushed the door open, he saw why.

Danny Foster lay on the floor of the room, trousers around his ankles. a girl in her late teens beneath him. She was completely naked and almost screamed when she saw Todd standing in the doorway.

Foster rolled off her and pulled his trousers up while the girl scrambled to her feet and tried to retrieve her clothes.

Todd looked around the room. At the worn sofa, the threadbare carpet, the empty bottles of beer scattered around. And, finally, he looked at the pimp and saw the hatred mirrored in the other man's eyes.

'What the fuck do you want?' he shouted. Then, seeing Vicki, he said, 'I told you what would happen if you kept on seeing this bastard.'

'Is that why you did that to her?' snarled Todd, pointing at the bruises around Vicki's eye.

'Keep your nose out of things that don't concern you,' Foster told him.

'They do concern me. What happens to Vicki matters to me.'

Foster laughed.

'How touching,' he sneered, then his tone hardened. 'She belongs to me. I own her. Now you get the fuck out of here before you get hurt.'

Todd shook his head.

'I'll go, but when I do, Vicki comes with me. Got it?'

Foster's face seemed to darken even more for a second and then he suddenly leapt at Todd, crashing into the reporter and knocking him off his feet. Both men rolled to one side, Todd scrambling to his knees, bringing one elbow down on the top of Foster's head. The pimp grunted and fell forward but, as he did, his left hand went to the back

136

pocket of his trousers and Todd heard the swish of the flick knife. He couldn't avoid the swipe and yelped in pain as it nicked his thigh. Blood spilled from the cut, staining his jeans and he got to his feet wincing.

Foster was on him in a flash but this time the wild swing missed and Todd managed to jump aside, bringing one foot up and catching the pimp in the groin. He crumpled up, clutching his testicles, his face a mask of pain and rage.

Vicki watched mesmerised as the two men squared up once more and Todd hastily grabbed one of the beer bottles, striking at Foster, catching him on the shoulder. The bottle broke and fell from the journalist's grasp. He ducked to avoid another pass with the knife but Foster struck out with his other hand too, a jolting blow which connected with Todd's jaw and sent him reeling. The reporter fell back, crashing into the coffee table as he did so. Foster advanced on him, the knife point gleaming wickedly in the dull light from the single lamp in the room. Todd shook his head, trying to clear the fuzziness. He grabbed the small table by two legs and swung it at the pimp. It slammed into him, the knife flying from his grasp, the table itself snapping in two. Todd found himself gripping a table leg, a convenient enough weapon because Foster had snatched up the second of the broken bottles and was waving the jagged glass prongs menacingly. He ducked forward, slashing out with the bottle, cutting Todd's hand but the journalist brought the table leg down on his opponent's skull, almost smiling when he heard the cracking of bone.

The pimp fell forward onto all fours, lashing out with one foot, tripping the journalist and bringing him down. But Todd rolled clear of the thrusting glass and smashed the wooden implement into Foster's face, shattering his nose. Foster dropped the broken bottle, blood pouring from his wound, his eyes watering, his head spinning. Todd, bleeding from the cuts on his thigh and hand hauled the pimp to his feet and glared into his eyes.

'If I ever see you again,' he rasped. 'I swear to Christ I'll kill you.' Then, with a grunt of satisfaction he drove a fist into Foster's face, the impact splitting his upper lip and loosening two front teeth. The pimp toppled over backwards, crashing over the sofa. He lay still, burbling incoherently.

Todd turned to Vicki who was staring down at the body of Foster. Then she looked up at him and he moved painfully across to her, wincing each time he put weight on his injured leg. Blood had formed a dark stain on his jeans and a burning sensation seemed to envelop the limb as he walked. But, supported by Vicki, he limped towards the door taking one last look at the prone figure of the pimp.

'Let's get out of here,' he said, wearily.

They sat in the hotel room without switching the light on and Todd lay back on the bed, the wound in his leg still throbbing. While he loosened his belt, Vicki soaked a towel in the sink. She wrung it out and returned to the bed, only now switching on the small lamp beside it. She looked at the slashed jeans, the stain looking black in the dull light and then at Todd who was easing the garment carefully down his leg wincing when he reached the wound. He felt stiff and when he pulled the jeans off, he yelped in pain. The blood had congealed, sticking the material to the ragged edges of the cut. It wasn't deep but it had bled a lot matting the hairs on his thigh, trickling down to his ankle. He sat up as Vicki began to sponge away the coagulated gore, gritting his teeth as she cleaned the wound itself. She returned to the sink twice to rinse the blood-soaked towel and, when his leg was cleaned up, Todd took the cloth from her and wiped the blood from his hand, exposing the two jagged lacerations just above his wrist.

He sat in his underpants, head bowed, the pain somehow lessened now that the cuts were cleaned up. He wrapped a handkerchief around his hand and Vicki found some plaster in her handbag but Todd declined. When they were taken off they would also take off most of the hairs on his thigh and, besides, the cut wasn't as bad as it looked.

'Are you all right, Dave?' Vicki asked him, watching as he rubbed his side.

'It only hurts when I laugh,' he said, smiling.

She knelt before him, hands resting on each of his knees. 'Thanks,' she said softly.

He reached out and touched her cheek, careful to avoid the swollen area around her right eye.

'Do you think he'll come looking for us?' she asked.

Todd shook his head.

'No.' There was an air of certainty in his voice which made her feel secure.

'What you said, about caring what happened to me? Did you mean it?' she asked.

'Do you think I'd have gone through that if I didn't?'

She swallowed hard.

'No. Did you really mean it? *Do* I mean that much to you? Foster could have killed you.'

He leant forward and kissed her on the forehead.

'Yes I did mean it,' he whispered. 'And yes, you do mean that much to me. Satisfied?'

He smiled and she raised herself to meet him, their mouths locking. She snaked her arms up around his neck, clutching him tightly to her, pressing her own body against his. As he felt her warmth and smelt the gorgeous scent of her body, despite his weariness, he felt the first stirrings of excitement in his groin. His hands fell to her breasts, squeezing them through the material then slowly, carefully, undoing the buttons until he could feel the taut flesh in his hands. She gasped and stroked the insides of his thighs, careful not to touch the cut but anxious to feel his stiffness.

She shrugged the blouse free and stood up, allowing him to kiss her breasts. He took each nipple in his mouth in turn, teasing them with his tongue until they grew into hard buds. He gripped her slim waist and fumbled with the button of her trousers, loosening them, pulling them over the round curve of her hips.

She sat down beside him and pulled off her boots, using her left foot to shuffle off the clinging satin trousers and finally, naked, she rolled onto her side, her eager hand gliding across his belly and down to his groin where she enveloped his rigid shaft with her gentle hand.

Todd, still lying on his back, swivelled around, his hands probing between her legs, feeling her moist and ready. She positioned herself above him, holding his penis with one hand, rotating her hips, allowing the bulbous head of his shaft to rub back and forth across her clitoris, then she guided it into her and impaled herself on his rampant organ. The movement made them both gasp and, for a second, she thought she had hurt him but Todd only let out a contented breath and raised his head. He gripped her waist as she moved up and down on him and he could feel the warmth of her body growing until it was a raging fire, a blaze of ecstasy between his legs. He held her close to him, his tongue flicking over her nipples as she moved more urgently, her own pleasure building. He sensed her gathering excitement and tensed his body, eager to reach a peak with her.

For long, glorious moments they were locked together, then Vicki began to shudder. She gripped his shoulders, grinding herself even harder against him, gasping her pleasure as she sank deeper onto his shaft. Todd also felt the unmistakable beginnings of orgasm and he lay back.

Vicki climaxed, almost screaming with the beauty of it. The feelings which swept through her made her quiver violently and she felt Todd release his own cascade into her, the sensation intensifying her own gratification. For what seemed like an eternity she remained in that position, eyes closed, chest heaving then she seemed to collapse onto his chest. He held her close, the perspiration from their bodies mingling.

'Oh God, that felt so good,' she murmured in his ear and she kissed him gently on the lips.

They lay together, clutching each other as if their lives depended upon it. Then her eyes opened and she gripped Todd almost painfully.

'Don't ever leave me, Dave,' she whispered, a note of pleading in her voice. 'Please.'

He shook his head.

'You try getting rid of me,' he grinned.

They embraced again, their bodies melting into one.

Twenty-three

'You were mine. You would have been mine forever if not for *him*.'

Edward spoke softly, his words subdued, as if they were actually having to cut through the thick rankness of the air in the bedroom. The stench was intolerable. Maureen's head was now in an advanced state of putrefaction, yellowish flakes of skin were beginning to peel away from the bones which strained against the taut flesh as if threatening to tear through it. The eyes looked like rotted boiled eggs, the eyeballs themselves having rolled upward in the sockets beneath the flabby lids.

He stood beside the bed, looking down at the head, breathing lungfuls of that foul air.

'I know what father must have felt like,' he said. 'I heard him that day. I saw what happened and it all happened because of another man. And because mother was weak. She betrayed father, he had no choice, he had to stop her leaving just as I had to stop you.' He turned away for a moment, the tone of his voice changing, there was a note of anger creeping in.

'Did you ever stop to think, just once, of how much I cared for you?'

The question hung on the reeking air.

'My love was deeper than *his* but you didn't want my love. You didn't care what *I* felt. I was something to be discarded.'

He turned back to face the head and his voice dropped in volume.

'These women I bring here are no better than you or mother were. They use men for money. They sell themselves. They don't care how disgusting that is, they don't care how degrading it is. They deserve to die.' He chuckled throatily. 'Rubbish is for disposing of and that is all they are. Rubbish.'

Again his tone changed and he dropped to his knees beside the head, touching one cold cheek with the back of his hand. It was like touching a dead fish and, as he drew closer, the stench seemed to fill not just his head but his entire body. He gazed into those sightless liquescent orbs as if expecting to see some glimmer of life there.

'I didn't want any of this to happen,' he moaned. 'Why did you have to try to leave me? Why?'

He lifted the head in both hands, staring at it.

'I loved you, Maureen and I still do. I always will.'

He drew the decomposing object closer to him until it was pressed against his face and then he planted his lips on the open mouth, kissing it deeply, tasting as well as smelling the decay. For interminable seconds he held it there, his tongue brushing over the bloodless lips, probing inside the mouth which was clogged with dried blood and other coagulated muck. Then, finally, he laid it down on the bed again. As he did so he felt his stomach churn and it was all he could do to prevent himself from vomiting. He dropped to his knees beside the bed once more gazing at the hacked off skull, his own saliva now on its crumbling flesh.

He grinned crookedly.

'But I enjoy being with those other women,' he said. 'The way you enjoyed being with *him*. They would do anything for money. Even die for it.' He began to laugh, the throaty chortling finally choking away as he wiped his mouth with the back of his hand.

'I think about them sometimes at nights,' he said. 'The way they dress, the way they behave. Showing themselves off. Tempting men to go with them. You and mother were no better. You were unpaid whores. You deserved to die just like they did.'

He stared at the head, as he knelt by the bed, his breath now coming in quick almost angry gasps.

'You should have been mine,' he roared. 'Mine!'

He lay down on the floor, gazing at the ceiling, listening to the gradually receding thud of his heart, the slow rasping of his breath.

'Whore,' he whispered.

Twenty-four

The alarm clock went off at eight a.m. and Todd thrust out a hand to shut off the persistent ringing. In the silence which followed he could hear the sounds of traffic outside and glancing across at the window he saw spots of rain on the unwashed glass.

Beside him, Vicki stirred, one hand reaching for him, brushing against his injured thigh as she did so. Todd yelped in pain and sat up. The leg ached and it felt as if he'd been kicked repeatedly in that one particular spot. As he swung himself out of bed and walked across to the dressing table, he felt some of the stiffness begin to wear off. He flexed the muscle, doing a couple of kneebends to ensure that it was all right. Watched by Vicki, he dressed then quickly ran an electric razor over his heavily stubbled cheeks and chin.

She sat up in bed, the sheets around her waist, arms resting on her knees.

'What will you do about getting your clothes from the house?' he asked her. 'I don't want you going back there.'

'One of the other girls will get them for me,' she told her. 'After what happened last night I don't think Danny will be too sorry to see the back of me.'

Todd grunted.

'So,' Vicki said. 'What next?'

'We try and find out where Penny and Amy have got to. Maureen Briggs as well, for that matter.'

Vicki looked puzzled.

'Maureen Briggs. But that's Edward's sister isn't it? She's at the house with him, surely.'

Todd told her what Fraser had told *him* the previous day.

'And she's been missing for a month?' Vicki said, sweeping a hand through her hair.

The journalist nodded.

'Of course,' he began. 'We still don't have any proof at all that Briggs is responsible for their disappearances.'

'Dave, for Christ's sake, he was the last one to be seen with them . . .'

He cut her short.

'As far as we know, he was. There's no proper evidence.'

'I thought *you* believed it too,' she said, looking hurt.

'I do,' he reassured her. 'But that still doesn't alter the fact that we don't have any concrete proof.'

'So what do we do? Call the police, hand it over to them?'

'No. We get the proof ourselves.'

'You mean go to the house?'

Todd crossed to the bed, pulling a piece of paper from his pocket as he did so. It bore the address of the Briggs' house.

'Going to the house wouldn't solve anything,' he said. 'Not just turning up on the doorstep anyway. What the hell are we going to say to him anyway? "Excuse me but what have you done with your sister and two prostitutes." That's not the way.'

'Then what the hell do we do?' Vicki demanded.

Todd exhaled deeply.

'He picks up pros because if they go missing there's no questions asked. No one gives a damn if one goes missing and nobody gets suspicious.'

'Tell me something I *don't* know,' she said, scornfully.

'He's not going to stop at two,' said Todd. 'Now, we don't know what he does with the girls once he gets them back to the house. We don't even know *if* he takes them back to the house.'

'Then how do we find out?' she wanted to know.

He looked directly at her, his gaze unwavering.

'*You* act as bait for him. Let him pick you up.'

146

She looked shocked but did not speak. Todd continued.

'Walk your beat just like you always used to, like Penny and Amy used to. If my hunch is right he'll be back sooner or later.'

'What if he picks up a different girl?' she said. 'There's scores of girls out there every night, why should he single me out?'

'We'll just have to hope he does,' Todd said.

'And *if* he does?'

There was silence for long moments then Todd crossed to the suitcase which he had pushed beneath the sideboard. He opened it and took out what looked like a tie-pin. He laid it on the bed and then retrieved a slim box-like console which was smaller than his hand. He held up the smaller of the two objects.

'It's a tracker,' he explained. 'I've used it before. When it's switched on,' he flicked a tiny switch at the base of the object, 'It gives off a signal that can be picked up on this.' He showed her the tiny console. There was a red light flashing on the grid which formed half of the slim box. It also gave off a strident beeping noise, rather like an oscilloscope. 'It's effective for about a mile,' he told her. 'Now, you clip this tracker somewhere on you, preferably inside your clothes, then if Briggs picks you up I can follow using the console.'

'As long as he doesn't get more than a mile in front of you,' said Vicki, cryptically.

'I can't think of any other way to do it,' the journalist confessed.

Vicki swallowed hard and held the tracker in her palm.

'Vicki, I won't lose you, I . . .'

She cut him short, raising a hand for him to be quiet.

'It's all right, Dave, I'll do it, you don't have to force me,' she said.

He gripped her free hand and squeezed.

'Everything will be OK,' he said, reassuringly. 'I'll be right behind you, don't worry.'

'What if we're wrong about Briggs?'

He shrugged.

'Then we're wrong but that still doesn't tell us where Penny and Amy are.'

She looked at the tracker once more then at Todd and he found it hard to hold her gaze.

'You want it to be true about Briggs don't you?' she said, almost accusingly and Todd swallowed hard, knowing she was right. 'You want a story. That's one of the reasons you've kept it from the police.'

He could look at her no longer.

'Nothing is going to go wrong,' he said, forcefully.

'You didn't answer my question,' she persisted. 'Are you using me to find the other girls or to get a good story?'

'I'm not using you, Vicki, I care too much for you to do that.'

'Then tell me the truth, Dave. You want a story out of this don't you?'

He nodded.

'Yes. I'm sorry you see it the way you do but . . .' he struggled to find the words. 'It is my living for Christ's sake. I'm sure Edward Briggs knows what happened to those three girls. He might even have killed them for all I know.'

'So you're going to use me as bait to catch a killer to prove your theory?'

'It's not like that,' he said, but he knew that what she said was true.

'Well, I said I'd do it. I will. You just make sure you keep within a mile of me once that bastard picks me up.'

Todd nodded.

'*If* I lose you,' he said, softly and Vicki raised her eyebrows in shock. 'I've got the address of the house.'

She wasn't convinced.

'And what if he doesn't take me back to the house? You said yourself you weren't sure he'd taken the other girls there.'

'There's nowhere else for him to go,' said Todd.

Vicki nodded wearily and clambered out of bed, reaching for her clothes. She dressed slowly then the two of them went out. They ate breakfast at a café about two hundred yards from the hotel but neither of them touched much food. Vicki in particular just prodded it with her knife and fork, content instead to down three cups of coffee and smoke a couple of cigarettes. Todd ate a rasher of bacon but little else. He cut his egg, watching the colour spill onto the plate then he put down the cutlery and looked at Vicki across the table.

She offered him a cigarette.

'What else did your policeman friend tell you about Edward Briggs?' she wanted to know.

Todd shrugged.

'Not much,' he said. 'He's got no criminal record of any sort, in fact Fraser told me that he seemed quite upset when he found out his sister had cleared off.'

Vicki nodded.

'Don't you think we'd better try out that toy of yours?' she said, pointing to the pocket where she knew Todd kept the tracker and its console. He took the transmitter from his pocket and handed it to her, watching as she clipped it to her blouse, inside the pocket. The red light on the console flared and he turned down the volume as the oscilloscopic blips began to sound.

She got to her feet.

'Walk about a bit,' he said. 'I'll give you ten minutes' start then follow.'

Vicki left him sitting in the café, drinking his second cup of coffee. He watched as the blip became fainter, the noise less strident but always audible.

Todd sucked hard on his cigarette and looked at his watch. It was 10.05 a.m. He wondered what time Briggs would arrive that night. If he arrived at all. Perhaps, Todd told himself, he was making too much of it. Perhaps his imagination was getting the better of him. He remembered when he'd first joined the paper, he'd done an article about a restaurant in Knightsbridge which had been found to have rats in one of its store rooms. Todd had written a damning piece about the place speculating on what other pests and horrors might be infesting the restaurant. His only evidence had been a piece of rat shit which he'd found beneath a work top. The editor of the paper had torn the article up and told him not to speculate, reminding him that facts were what mattered.

'You're a journalist, not a bloody novelist,' the editor had shouted at him. 'Don't use your imagination. Use what facts you have.'

Now Todd stared into his coffee cup and made a mental note of the few facts he did have. And, when the inventory was completed, he realized that it added up to sod all. There wasn't one concrete piece of evidence linking Edward Briggs to the disappearance of Penny and Amy other than the fact they'd been seen getting into his car. Todd was working on supposition. A hunch. A gut feeling. Whichever cliché he cared to use, it was all he had.

He looked at his watch again and got to his feet, paid the bill on the way out and then took the console from his pocket and set about finding Vicki.

It took him fifteen minutes.

The tracker worked.

Todd spent the rest of the day in the hotel room, putting the finishing touches to his piece on vice, the article which he had originally come to do. He read it two or three times scanning the manuscript impassively.

Vicki went to see a friend of hers who said she would go to the house in Earlham street and get her clothes for her. The other girl returned with the stuff in a large brown suitcase which Vicki humped back to the hotel.

She changed into fresh clothes and Todd made sure that the transmitter was firmly attached to her coat, secreted in an inside pocket. Neither of them spoke very often or very much and, as Todd held her close to him, he could feel her heart beating faster than usual.

'Frightened?' he said.

'What do you think?' Vicki answered.

Todd went to his car and brought it round to the front of the hotel then he returned to the room. Vicki was lighting up another cigarette, grinding it out before it was even half finished. He crossed to the window and looked out.

'What now?' she asked.

'We wait,' said Todd.

Outside, the last dying rays of the sun were staining the heavens an ominous crimson as evening drove back the daylight.

Todd looked at his watch.

It was 7.46 p.m.

Twenty-five

The sky above looked overcast, dark banks of rain cloud scudding across the already black backdrop, threatening to unleash a deluge at any moment. Edward Briggs unlocked the driver's door of the Dolomite and slid behind the wheel. The engine started first time and he pulled out into the street, swinging the vehicle round in the direction of Central London.

Haloes seemed to have formed around the street lamps which had just burst into life, their sodium glow soon to be replaced by the myriad neon explosions which marked the city centre.

Edward felt a curious kind of exhilaration as he drove, scanning the pavements on either side of him as he threaded his way through traffic.

Two or three large spots of rain hit the windscreen and he flicked on the wipers, watching as the rubber blades brushed the water away. The deluge looked as if it had started but, after a few minutes, the screen cleared again and Edward found that he could switch off the wipers.

He smiled thinly to himself, his sense of excitement growing as he reached the first of the sign posts which would lead him to what had become a hunting ground. The neon lights flashed all around him, the very air itself crackling with energy.

Edward glanced at his watch.

8.56 p.m.

Vicki was standing in the doorway of the Venus, looking across at Todd who was seated behind the wheel of his blue

Chevette. On the passenger seat beside him was the console, the red light on it glowing fiercely, the blip sounding loud in the confines of the car. On the parcel shelf was the piece of paper which bore the address of the Briggs' house.

The journalist looked at his watch for the last time then he looked across at Vicki and nodded.

She immediately began walking.

Todd watched her as she made her way through the crowds thronging Shaftesbury Avenue, the beep from the tracker still loud. He let her get out of sight then turned the key in the ignition. The engine roared but didn't start and Todd muttered something to himself.

He tried again.

Still nothing.

'Come on you bastard,' he rasped, pulling out the choke as far as it would go, simultaneously pressing his foot gently onto the accelerator.

This time the engine spluttered into life. The journalist breathed an audible sigh of relief, let it warm up for a moment or two then pulled out into the traffic.

The beeping of the console continued at a steady pitch.

Edward was in the process of parking the Dolomite when he saw the tall coloured girl walking towards him. She was wearing silver eye-shadow which seemed to catch and diffuse the numerous colours of the lights around her. She wobbled precariously on a pair of red stilettos. Edward watched her as she approached the car, her heavily painted lips sliding back like some kind of ruby trap door to reveal a row of pearl white teeth.

She stood on the pavement watching him as he parked. He shut off the engine and got out.

But, as he approached her, the expression of welcome changed to one of horror and she turned her back on him, retreating into the club behind her. Edward was puzzled but, as he turned he saw a police car drive slowly past, both the driver and passenger vigilantly scanning the pavements and doorways.

Edward waited until the car had passed then he wandered along the street towards a place called 'Kiss and Tell'. It displayed its name in bulbs of bright pink, three or four of which had blown and the interrupted display reminded him of a row of broken teeth. Edward paid his money at the door and went inside. He nearly stumbled in the dull light and it took him a moment or two to become accustomed to the gloom. As his eyes cleared he found that he was descending a narrow staircase. At the bottom were two heavy curtains, thick with dust and worn at the sides which, when opened, led into a room with about half a dozen tables, a bar and, at the far end, a stage.

Two girls, one clad in a leather leotard, thigh boots and leather studded wristbands which went as far as her elbow and another in just a torn cotton T-shirt, were dancing. They pressed close together, occasionally kissing, moving slowly in time to the music which was deafening.

Smoke billowed in front of the stage, curling and twisting in the coloured spotlights which picked out each girl.

Edward went to a table close to the stage and sat down, eyes fixed on the sight before him.

As he watched, the leather clad girl took a rope from around her waist and tied the other girl's wrists together. The one in the T-shirt, a little blonde with large breasts and a mole on her left thigh, pretended to be in pain and Edward watched, mesmerised, as a cross-shaped object rose from the stage itself. The girl in leather then bound her companion to this cross. After ensuring that her 'victim' was securely tied, the leather clad girl left the stage briefly, only to return with a large vibrator.

Unable to control himself, Edward felt his erection throbbing against the inside of his trousers and he smiled as he saw the blonde squirming with fake delight as the mock phallus was drawn across her body.

* * *

Vicki shivered and looked at her watch.

10.23 p.m.

She had been standing around for over two hours now. Her feet ached and she was cold. She pulled her coat tighter, careful not to dislodge the transmitter. She wondered what Todd was doing. At least he was in the warm, while she was stuck out on the street in the biting wind, waiting for the next downpour. The sky was mottled, thick with cloud and she wondered how much longer it would be before the rain came. She sighed. It was like waiting for a bomb to go off. Only in this case it was a bomb that had probably not even been primed. She knew the chances of Edward Briggs turning up were pretty good but *her* chances of finding him and of being picked up by him she didn't care to think about. She decided to wander up and down in the hope of spotting him, or at least the car.

Two other men had tried to pick her up already that night but she refused, thinking how ironic it was that now she could tell them where to go instead of having to worry about what that little shit Danny was going to say when she got back.

She smiled thinly to herself and crossed the road.

The white Dolomite almost hit her.

Vicki spun round, the headlamps glaring in her eyes and, it was a second or two before she realized that it was *that* car which had almost knocked her down.

Edward was already clambering out of the driver's seat, walking around to the front of the car, his eyes appraising her as she approached.

She swallowed hard as he drew closer. So, this was Briggs. Vicki wondered if this was how Amy had felt when she'd been with him, whether she had broken out into the same cold sweat which seemed to envelop Vicki as the man came towards her.

'I didn't see you,' he said.

'It was my fault,' she replied. 'I should have been looking where I was going.'

'Are you hurt?' he wanted to know and she shuddered as she felt his eyes upon her.

She winced as she put her foot down, feigning injury.

'I think it's my ankle,' she lied. 'Perhaps you could give me a lift. I'd be grateful. If you get my drift.'

He did.

'Get in,' he told her and she hobbled around to the passenger side.

'You're not really hurt are you?' he said, accusingly.

She shrugged.

'Well, no, but it's best not to advertise your business in the middle of the street isn't it?' The smile she managed was only by monumental effort. I know a place we can go if . . .'

He cut her short.

'I'll pay you extra if you'll stay with me the night. At my house.'

Vicki swallowed hard.

'OK,' she said, as cheerfully as possible. 'But it'll cost you an extra fifty.'

'I know,' Edward intoned icily. 'That's what the others said.'

Almost unconsciously, Vicki touched the transmitter and prayed that Todd was close by.

The journalist sat up as he noticed the change of pitch in the sound coming from the console. He realized that it was because Vicki was moving faster. She *had* to be in a car. He took a deep breath and pushed the Chevette up a gear, scanning the traffic around and in front of him as he followed the direction of the ever present blips. The signal indicated that Vicki was not too far off but the sooner he had that bloody Dolomite in view the better he thought. He drove without taking his eyes off the road for one second, alert for the slightest glimpse of his quarry's car.

He was in Tottenham Court Road by now and the traffic was jammed thickly in both directions. Todd banged on his hooter as a yellow Mini momentarily blocked his way. Then, still alert, he drove on, hardly noticing that a small bead of perspiration had appeared on his forehead. Soon it was joined by others.

His heart began to thud just that little bit faster against his ribs and he blinked hard to clear his eyes which seemed to have misted over but he realized that it was just the effect of gazing at so much light. It poured in from all directions. The white light of headlamps, the fiery red of brake lights, neon signs erupting in rainbow cascades, all conspiring against him it seemed. Intent on thwarting his attempts to spot the elusive Dolomite.

The blips from the console continued with their steady rhythm.

'Come on, come on,' he muttered, his voice coming out as a hollow croak.

A white car pulled out just ahead of him and Todd looked at it in surprise.

'Shit,' he rasped, banging the steering wheel angrily when he saw that it was an old Triumph.

The blips seemed to be growing louder but still he could not see the vehicle he sought.

Vicki shuffled uncomfortably in her seat and studied Edward's profile. He was a little older than Todd she guessed, not unattractive but there was something darkly sinister about his square, hard features. She wondered whether or not she would have thought that about him had she not known that he'd been responsible for the disappearance and probable death of two of her friends. The car smelt of stale perfume.

'Do you do this sort of thing often?' she said, smiling. 'This car smells like a mobile brothel.'

He didn't answer.

She sucked in another troubled breath and resisted the urge to turn around. God, how she longed to look out of the rear window and see Todd's Chevette behind them but she resisted the temptation.

'You didn't tell me your name,' she said.

'Does it matter?' Edward muttered.

'I'm curious.'

He told her.

Confirmation of what she already knew only served to make her more nervous and she glanced into one of the wing mirrors but all she saw was a blur of headlamps.

'Where are we going?' she asked him.

'My house,' he said. 'I told you.'

She nodded.

'So you did.'

This time she didn't even try to laugh.

The blips from the console seemed to fill the car, reaching deafening proportions, and Todd smiled as he finally caught sight of the white Dolomite. It was two lanes across from him, he could afford to waste no time. A quick glance in his rear-view mirror and he swung the Chevette over. This particular manoeuvre was greeted by a chorus of hooter blasts and shouts of anger from drivers behind and he almost collided with a taxi as he eased the vehicle into lane about two car lengths from the elusive Dolomite. He could see the back of Vicki's head, noticing how she would turn every so often to say something to Briggs who remained hunched over the wheel without so much as a sideways glance at her.

Todd felt a little easier now that he actually had the car in sight but he still drove with his fists gripping the wheel until they were bloodless. He wondered what he would do when he actually caught up with Briggs. More to the point, how was Briggs himself going to react? The questions tumbled through his mind as he sped along after the Dolomite which was now leaving the heart of London, the traffic thinning into two lanes.

Todd kept his eyes fixed firmly on the other vehicle, touching his own brake as he saw the tail lights on the Dolomite flare.

There were traffic lights ahead.

Briggs drove through but Todd realized with horror that he was not going to make it before they turned red. He thought about putting his foot down and shooting through them but he realized that his quarry might think something was strange if a car went through a red light to keep up with him.

The journalist slammed on his brakes, watching the cyclopic eye of the traffic lights, then peering hard at the Dolomite which was receding into the distance, the blips from the console becoming a little fainter.

After what seemed like an eternity, the lights changed and Todd stepped on the accelerator with such vehemence that the wheels spun impotently on the road for long seconds, leaving thick tread marks. There was a high pitched shriek as the rubber burned on the tarmac and then the Chevette shot forward once more. The reporter drove as fast as he dared, looking ahead once more, relaxing a little when the beeping grew louder, telling him that he was close. And, indeed, a moment or two later, he could see the Dolomite again.

The lorry pulled out from the side turning with no warning at all. It emerged from the darkness like some prehistoric monster, just its side lights glinting. And it was a big bastard too.

'Jesus,' shrieked Todd and spun the wheel, simultaneously hitting his brakes, praying that the car wouldn't turn over. The lorry driver too tried to avoid the collision and twisted the wheel of the juggernaut in time to avoid contact between car and cab, but the Chevette spun round and smacked hard into the side of the lorry. It was piled high with wood, covered with tarpaulin and, despite the thick securing chains, the impact set the load swaying. As Todd watched one of the chains broke loose, whiplashing as it was torn free of its securing lock. The wood tottered precariously for long moments then fell sideways into the road, some of the thick planks cracking as they hit the ground.

The driver was already out of his cab, watching helplessly as his load spilled from the lorry.

Todd leapt out of his car.

'Can't you move this bloody thing?' he yelled.

'And where do you suggest I move it to?' the driver said, shaken by the near collision. 'If you hadn't come teararsing down here at such a fucking speed this wouldn't have happened.'

'Maybe if you'd looked before you pulled out,' Todd replied, challengingly.

'Oh sod it,' the driver said, dejectedly. 'The bloody road's blocked. That's it.' He waved a hand towards the mountain of wood which had spilled across the street.

People in the houses on either side had come out to their front doors or were peering out of windows to see what had happened and a jam of other vehicles had formed on either side of the stricken juggernaut.

Todd turned and ran back to his car.

'Oi, where the bleedin' hell are you going?' shouted the lorry driver. 'I've got to call the old Bill, report this. I need you as a witness.'

Todd started his engine.

'*You* tell them what happened,' he said and turned the car in a sharp U, heading towards a side street, hoping that it would bring him back onto the main road beyond the scene of the accident.

The blips coming from the console were now almost inaudible and, as he picked it up, the red light, which not long ago had been flashing so brightly, now barely flickered. Todd threw it down onto the passenger seat, his breath coming in gasps, his entire body now sheathed in sweat.

By the time he swung the car back onto the main road the console was silent.

He shook it, hoping that it might be a malfunction but he

160

knew only too well that he had lost the Dolomite. He had the address of the Briggs' house and, from his present position, he guessed that it would take him perhaps thirty minutes to reach it.

He looked at his watch and floored the accelerator.

It was 11.32 p.m.

Twenty-six

Vicki shuddered involuntarily as she watched Edward Briggs turn the key in the front door and, as he motioned her inside, she recoiled from the powerful odour which hit her. It was like stepping into an open sewer. The smell, whatever it was, seemed to be emanating from the very walls themselves and Vicki coughed. It smelt like very old, bad, cabbage. However, after a moment or two, she regained control and looked around the hall. She noted stairs to her right, the cellar door and, beyond it, the short darkened corridor which led to the sitting room and dining room, each joined by connecting doors. She noted with curiosity that there were keys in the locks of every one.

As she took another step into the house she stumbled and almost fell over something, looking down she saw that it was a long leather hold-all of some description. It was partly undone and she glimpsed the pointed end of a screw driver jutting out.

'My tool bag,' Edward said, monosyllabically, moving the offending object aside.

Vicki nodded, smiled thinly and took another pace ahead of him, as if anxious to keep some distance between the two of them.

Consequently, she had her back turned when Edward locked the front door, dropping the key into his jacket pocket.

He led Vicki into the sitting room, where the nauseating stench she had first encountered was replaced, in some way, by the smell of damp. Edward pointed to the sofa and she sat down.

'It's quiet in here,' she said.

He chuckled.

'As quiet as the grave, as they say.'

Vicki felt the hairs rise on the back of her neck.

'The house is sound-proofed,' he told her. 'No noise gets in or out.'

She nodded, looking around the spacious sitting room, her eyes finally coming to rest on the photo of Maureen.

'Is that your sister?' she said.

'How did you know?' he snapped.

'There's a resemblance,' Vicki lied. 'Just a guess.'

'Yes, it is my sister. We live here together.'

'And she doesn't mind you bringing girls back to the house?'

He ignored the question.

'Isn't this the time when you ask me what I'd like?' he said, his voice thick with scorn.

'What you'd like?' she said, puzzled.

'The others asked. One of them reeled off quite a list.'

Vicki sucked in a low breath.

'Look, there's no hurry. If I'm staying the night, we don't have to rush.'

Edward eyed her suspiciously.

'You said there'd been others,' Vicki began. 'What did your sister have to say about them?'

'We have an understanding,' he said.

Vicki nodded, her heart hammering against her ribs like a pile-driver.

'You mean you bring girls back and she brings men back. Is that it?'

'No, that isn't it,' he growled. 'She isn't interested in other men.'

Vicki could feel her body trembling and she was having difficulty disguising it.

Then, suddenly, his mood relaxed and that crooked smile spread across his face again. Vicki found it even more unsettling than his anger.

'I'll let you meet her,' he said, softly.

Vicki looked surprised.

'You mean she's here, now?'

'Come with me,' he instructed and led her out of the sitting room towards the stair. Vicki followed obediently, eyes straying briefly to her watch. Where the hell had Todd got to she wondered? Once in the hall, her nostrils were assaulted by that rank, fetid odour which she had first encountered on entering the house but now, as she ascended the stairs with Edward, it seemed to grow stronger until she could barely stand it. Like a cloud of noxious gas it swirled around her and she coughed again. She saw the four doors before her. Each one was closed.

Edward crossed to one and turned a key in the lock. He stood proudly by the door and motioned for her to join him, which she did, the smell now completely overpowering.

'My sister,' he proclaimed.

As if invisible tentacles were encircling her throat, Vicki found that her scream was choked back but, from somewhere deep within her, she found that breath and shrieked at the monstrosity which confronted her.

Maureen's head had almost completely decayed. What little flesh remained was yellow, mottled green around the nose and sunken eyes. Those orbs themselves were like putrescing boiled eggs. The hair had begun to come away in untidy hunks and it lay on the bed along with the pieces of skin which had peeled off, leaving just crumbling bone beneath. There were even three or four teeth lying amidst the other debris.

Vicki felt her head spinning, her stomach churning and she thought she was going to faint but suddenly, Edward was at her, clamping both hands around her neck in a vice-like grip. The muscles in his arms bulged as he tightened his hold, squeezing until it felt as if someone had secured a steel collar around her throat. Vicki's eyes bulged in their sockets, her face turning the colour of dark grapes as she fought for her breath. Edward grunted and she actually felt herself being lifted bodily into the air, supported by those hands but dying because of them. A red mist began to cloud her vision and she felt Edward pressing his thumbs even tighter into her windpipe, his face just inches from her own.

With her last ounce of strength she reached out and drove two long-nailed fingers into his left eye, raking the flesh above and below, splitting the bottom eyelid. She felt the blood spurt onto her hand and Edward's scream of agony drummed loud in her ears.

The grip around her throat relaxed and he dropped her like an unwanted doll, clutching at the shredded skin of his face. She crawled away as he bellowed like a wounded bull, the crimson liquid trickling through his fingers. It felt as if his face were on fire and he staggered about blindly for long seconds.

Vicki gasped and massaged her throat, finding it difficult to swallow. She coughed and bloodied mucous welled over her lips. She managed to haul herself upright and, using the bannister to support her weight she hurried down the stairs as best she could

Edward shouted something at her and came after her, grunting madly.

Vicki quickened her pace and reached the bottom of the stairs, grabbing at the handle of the front door which she found was locked. She almost screamed aloud, more in despair than anything else and, looking round, she saw Edward careering down the stairs, his face a torn, dark mask of hatred.

Vicki spun round and dashed down the short corridor towards the sitting room. She slowed her pace then, moving carefully in the darkness, trying to find her way to the kitchen and, maybe, an escape route through the back door.

Edward dropped to his knees as he reached the hall. He wrenched open his tool bag and pulled out a hatchet, hefting the viciously sharp, three pound tool before him for a moment. Then, he got up and walked quietly into the sitting room. The only sound was his guttural breathing as he moved into the room, electing to leave the lights off. He enjoyed the darkness and the silence inside the house.

This was a new game for him. There was no way for the girl to escape.

In the kitchen, Vicki struggled to control her own breathing, terrified that even the slightest sound would alert Edward and bring him to her. She crept across the kitchen, taking a large knife from the rack as she went. The back door was just ahead of her, another door to the left of that.

She took one quick look behind her and tugged on the handle of the back door.

It was locked.

Still clutching the knife she turned to the other door. There was a key in it and, when she turned it, she found herself in the corridor once more. The silence seemed to suffocate her as she moved along the narrow carpeted lobby towards another door. That too had a key in the lock and, looking around, Vicki turned it.

It was stiff and creaked alarmingly as it turned. Cursing under her breath she took the key from the lock, stepped inside the room and re-locked it.

She had to use every ounce of self-control to prevent herself vomiting. The stench which she had encountered in the bedroom upstairs seemed insignificant set against the palpable fetidness of the air in this particular room. The effect was dizzying and she put out a hand to steady herself, seeking a light switch for the darkness was impenetrable. She realized that the curtains were closed in this room. She was blind. Holding the knife in one hand, she clamped the other over her nose and mouth, taking small shallow breaths to minimise the revolting intensity of the smell. It was ten times worse than before.

But, slowly, as her eyes became accustomed to the darkness, she could make out a dark shape near the window.

Her heart missed a beat, the breath catching in her throat.

Had Edward managed to get into the room before her?

She stood still for long seconds then, carefully, retreated, tracing her path along the wall until she found the light switch. Gratefully, she flicked it on. Then, realizing that he would be able to see the strip of light beneath the door she hurriedly turned it off again and was plunged once more into that infinity of blackness. But, in those split seconds of light, she had been able to see that dark shape at the far end of the room hadn't been Edward. She moved slowly across the carpet, towards the curtains which she then carefully pulled back.

What little natural light there was poured in and, she could actually see what she was doing.

There was a large sideboard in the room and, beside that, the carpet had been pulled up and a number of floor boards removed. She crossed to the other side of the room, anxious to discover what secret lay hidden there. As she reached it, the moon fought its way out from behind the cloying banks of cloud and flooded the room with light.

In the cold glow, Vicki looked down.

There were two bodies down there, both of which looked vaguely familiar. But these abominations which lay before her, mutilated beyond recognition, one of them with eyes completely gone, could not be who she thought they were. Could they?

'Penny?' she whimpered. 'Amy?'

She saw the gold cross around the neck of the first corpse and realized that she was, indeed, looking at the remains of what had once been her friends. They couldn't have looked worse if they'd been through a mincing machine. The skin was decaying, like the head upstairs. A choking smell rose from the hole.

Vicki backed away, crashing into a table then the sideboard. There was something sticking out of one drawer and it was a second or two before she realized that it was a human hand. She knelt and opened the doors.

The remains of Maureen Briggs' headless body tumbled out and lay at her feet.

Vicki could contain herself no longer. She screamed as loud as she could, staggering backwards until she fell over the dark shape near the window. She sprawled on the floor beside it, her hands touching polythene. It was a man's body. Or at least what was left of a man. His eyes were open, fixing her in a malevolent stare and she screamed once more.

Outside the door she heard movement and, as she struggled to her feet, she heard Edward's voice.

He was shouting something, rattling the door handle in his efforts to gain entry.

Vicki looked around for a means of escape, finding that the window was also locked. She looked around for something to break the glass with but, as she did so, she heard the first blows of the hatchet as Edward began hacking his way through the door to reach her.

Twenty-seven

Todd spotted the Dolomite parked in the driveway of the house and was thankful that at least he knew where Briggs and Vicki were. Whether he was in time or not was another matter.

He stepped on the brake, the car skidding to a halt. The journalist leapt out, slipping over as he did so, but he scrambled to his feet and ran towards the house, vaulting the low fence which marked the perimeter of the garden. He spotted the doors to the cellar bulkhead immediately and scuttled towards them.

A padlock and chain held them firmly shut.

'Bastard,' rasped Todd and tugged ineffectively at the chain. He turned and saw several large pieces of rock lying nearby. He picked one up and began slamming it down on the padlock, using all his strength. The metal finally gave and he tore the chain free. He wrenched open the doors, finding himself at the top of a flight of stone steps which led down into the gloom of the cellar. He descended quickly, the doors slamming shut behind him, and Todd was struck by the silence. Then that solitude was shattered as he heard the sound of screams, punctuated by that of splintering wood.

'Vicki,' he gasped and looked around, snatching a claw hammer from a rack on the wall. He dashed up the stairs which would take him into the hall but, as he tugged on the handle, he found that it too was locked.

Todd began striking it with the hammer.

* * *

Vicki could only stand mesmerised as she watched Edward cleave his way through the door. First one panel, then another were crushed under the impact of the repeated blows. Only when she actually saw the razor sharp head of the hatchet burst through into the room did she find the strength to move. She ran to the door, striking out randomly with the knife as he tried to smash his way in. She succeeded in cutting his hand, almost shouting aloud as she saw the blood burst from the gash but it didn't seem to stop him and he now concentrated his attention on the lock itself. Under such concerted strength it couldn't stand for long and, as Vicki watched, shaking her head slowly from side to side, Edward smashed the lock and kicked open what remained of the door.

He stood there, framed by the cold white light of the moon, a vision from hell. His hands splashed with blood, half of his face torn by her nails. The hatchet gripped in one fist.

'Whore,' he shouted.

But then it was his turn to freeze as he heard the cellar door being tugged open.

He turned away from Vicki and she realized what was happening.

'Vicki.'

She recognised Todd's voice.

She could not find the breath to answer him.

Edward moved away from the door, raising the axe and Todd gripped the hammer tighter. Briggs was bigger than he'd first thought and, for some reason, Fraser's words flashed into his mind – 'No heroics'. The journalist was breathing heavily, aware also of the vile stench in the building. He backed up a pace and steadied himself.

'You dared break into my house,' said Briggs, through clenched teeth. Then, suddenly, he ran at Todd, bringing the hatchet down with terrifying force, missing the journalist by inches. For his own part, Todd spun round and slammed the hammer into Edward's side. There was a harsh crack of bone as one rib was broken and the journalist threw himself clear in an effort to avoid the second swing of the axe. This time he wasn't so quick and the razor-sharp blade ripped through the leather of his jacket and cut his right arm from shoulder to elbow. Blood burst from the savage wound and Todd yelped in pain as he felt the limb go numb. He rolled over, switching the hammer to his other hand as Edward advanced again.

Todd ducked beneath the swing and lashed out with the hammer, shouting victoriously as the twin claws buried themselves in Edward's shoulder. But, as the other man fell, he pulled the hammer from Todd's grasp and the journalist found himself defenceless. He watched as Edward tore the claws free from his shoulder, holding the dripping hammer in one hand, the axe in the other.

The journalist knew he had no choice.

Edward had his back to the open cellar door, Todd launched himself at the killer and drove his shoulder into Edward's chest. Edward grunted, the wind knocked from him, the impact lifting him off his feet. He crashed down the steps and lay still at the bottom, blood dripping from a nasty gash on the forehead. Todd turned away from the door, clutching his lacerated arm.

'Vicki,' he called.

She emerged from the dining room, the knife still clutched in her hand, face as pale as milk.

'Thank God you're alive,' he whispered.

She crossed to him, seeing just how bad the cut on his arm was. Blood was pumping from the rent in thick streams and the journalist's face was waxen.

'He did kill the others,' said Vicki. 'They're in there.' She motioned behind her and Todd nodded.

'Call the police and an ambulance,' he said, returning to the cellar doorway.

Edward still lay motionless at the bottom of the steps, the hammer and knife discarded. Todd heard Vicki dialling as he slapped on the light and descended into the subterranean cavern. He felt sick but he forced himself to bend, inspecting Edward's prone form.

A hand snaked up and grabbed him by the hair, pulling

his head down hard. Taken by surprise, Todd could not defend himself and, his head smacked hard against one of the steps. He groaned and rolled over, watching as Edward scrambled to his feet and scuttled across the cellar to a cupboard. Todd saw him wrench the door open, take something out and, a second later, he heard the roar of the chainsaw as Edward advanced upon him.

Upstairs, Vicki heard it too and dropped the phone racing to the cellar door in time to see Edward swinging the lethal weapon around gleefully. Todd got to his feet and backed off. He knelt and picked up the hammer again, realizing he would have no chance if Edward got close. The din from the McCullough was deafening.

Edward lunged but Todd side-stepped and hit him hard on the back of the neck with the blunt end of the hammer. It staggered him and Todd snatched up a long length of wood from the pile nearby. At least he could keep his opponent at a distance with it. Or so he thought. The wood must have been at least six inches thick but the chainsaw sliced through it as if it were balsa wood and Todd found himself pinned in a corner, with his attacker drawing nearer by the second.

Vicki ran down the stairs and snatched up the hatchet, holding it in both hands to steady herself.

Todd had just two feet of wood left between himself and the snarling barbs of the McCullough and he could see Edward's triumphant, bloodied, face distorted into a snarl of victory.

A snarl which, a second later, turned to a look of agony.

Using all her strength, Vicki buried the axe between the madman's shoulder blades, tearing it free only to drive it into him again, so deeply that the razor edged blade slashed open a lung. Blood sprayed from the wounds and spattered her and Todd saw his attacker's eyes roll upward in their sockets as more thick crimson fluid flooded over his lips.

Edward staggered for a second then dropped the chainsaw. Unable to stop himself, he fell forward onto the churning blade.

Todd jumped clear as the other man's scream filled the

air. The McCullough bit through his chest and stomach, releasing a tangle of entrails, boring further, through the lungs which gave way with a loud, liquid burst. Then, as Edward squirmed frenziedly, seemingly pinned on the roaring chainsaw, the blade finally ate through his scapula, scything away one arm, effectively cutting the body in two length-ways. Gobbets of flesh and huge gouts of blood erupted upwards and splashed into Todd's face. He held onto Vicki who was screaming, as if trying to drown out the sound of the roaring chainsaw, as the crimson fountains continued to spurt high into the air and the lethal device caused Edward's corpse to move about like some kind of writhing eel. There was a final explosion of blood and excrement from the body and then it was still. Todd stooped and switched the machine off.

In the silence which followed, they could both hear blood dripping from the corpse.

Supported by Vicki, Todd struggled back up the stairs to the hall, shutting the cellar door behind him. Both of them were drenched with blood and Vicki had to wipe her hands on her skirt before she could pick the phone up to call for help.

Todd closed his eyes and listened as she called an ambulance and the police. Then they both waited, huddled together like two children who have been through a shared nightmare.

'No heroics,' said Todd, softly.

'What did you say?' Vicki asked, holding him, allowing him to snake his good arm around her.

'Fraser told me not to be a hero,' he said and coughed.

'I didn't think you were going to get here in time,' she told him, her eyes full of tears.

He smiled thinly.

'You know, you're going to have to learn to trust me,' he croaked.

She smiled but that smile dissolved into a flood of tears. And he held her tight.

The sound of sirens began to fill the night.

STAR BOOKS BESTSELLERS

THRILLERS

OUTRAGE	*Henry Denker*	£1.95 ☐
FLIGHT 902 IS DOWN	*H Fisherman &*	£1.95 ☐
	B. Schiff	
TRAITOR'S EXIT	*John Gardner*	£1.60 ☐
ATOM BOMB ANGEL	*Peter James*	£1.95 ☐
HAMMERED GOLD	*W.O. Johnson*	£1.95 ☐
DEBT OF HONOUR	*Adam Kennedy*	£1.95 ☐
THE FIRST DEADLY SIN	*Laurence Sanders*	£2.60 ☐
KING OF MONEY	*Jeremy Scott*	£1.95 ☐
DOG SOLDIERS	*Robert Stone*	£1.95 ☐

CHILLERS

SLUGS	*Shaun Hutson*	£1.60 ☐
THE SENTINEL	*Jeffrey Konvitz*	£1.65 ☐
OUIJA	*Andrew Laurance*	£1.50 ☐
HALLOWEEN III	*Jack Martin*	£1.80 ☐
PLAGUE	*Graham Masterton*	£1.80 ☐
MANITOU	*Graham Masterton*	£1.80 ☐
SATAN'S LOVE CHILD	*Brian McNaughton*	£1.35 ☐
DEAD AND BURIED	*Chelsea Quinn Yarbo*	£1.75 ☐

STAR Books are obtainable from many booksellers and newsagents. If you have any difficulty tick the titles you want and fill in the form below.

Name_____

Address_____

_____

Send to: Star Books Cash Sales, P.O. Box 11, Falmouth, Cornwall. TR10 9EN.

Please send a cheque or postal order to the value of the cover price plus:
UK: 45p for the first book, 20p for the second book and 14p for each additional book ordered to the maximum charge of £1.63.

BFPO and EIRE: 45p for the first book, 20p for the second book, 14p per copy for the next 7 books, thereafter 8p per book.

OVERSEAS: 75p for the first book and 21p per copy for each additional book.

While every effort is made to keep prices low, it is sometimes necessary to increase prices at short notice. Star Books reserve the right to show new retail prices on covers which may differ from those advertised in the text or elsewhere.

STAR BOOKS BESTSELLERS

FICTION

WAR BRIDES	*Lois Battle*	£2.50 ☐
AGAINST ALL GODS	*Ashley Carter*	£1.95 ☐
THE STUD	*Jackie Collins*	£1.75 ☐
SLINKY JANE	*Catherine Cookson*	£1.35 ☐
THE OFFICERS' WIVES	*Thomas Fleming*	£2.75 ☐
THE CARDINAL SINS	*Andrew M. Greeley*	£1.95 ☐
WHISPERS	*Dean R. Koontz*	£1.95 ☐
LOVE BITES	*Molly Parkin*	£1.60 ☐
GHOSTS OF AFRICA	*William Stevenson*	£1.95 ☐

NON-FICTION

BLIND AMBITION	*John Dean*	£1.50 ☐
DEATH TRIALS	*Elwyn Jones*	£1.25 ☐
A WOMAN SPEAKS	*Anaïs Nin*	£1.60 ☐
I CAN HELP YOUR GAME	*Lee Trevino*	£1.60 ☐
TODAY'S THE DAY	*Jeremy Beadle*	£2.95 ☐

BIOGRAPHY

IT'S A FUNNY GAME	*Brian Johnston*	£1.95 ☐
WOODY ALLEN	*Gerald McKnight*	£1.75 ☐
PRINCESS GRACE	*Gwen Robyns*	£1.75 ☐
STEVE OVETT	*Simon Turnbull*	£1.80 ☐
EDDIE: MY LIFE, MY LOVES	*Eddie Fisher*	£2.50 ☐

STAR Books are obtainable from many booksellers and newsagents. If you have any difficulty tick the titles you want and fill in the form below.

Name_____

Address_____

_____

Send to: Star Books Cash Sales, P.O. Box 11, Falmouth, Cornwall. TR10 9EN.

Please send a cheque or postal order to the value of the cover price plus:
UK: 45p for the first book, 20p for the second book and 14p for each additional book ordered to the maximum charge of £1.63.

BFPO and EIRE: 45p for the first book, 20p for the second book, 14p per copy for the next 7 books, thereafter 8p per book.

OVERSEAS: 75p for the first book and 21p per copy for each additional book.

While every effort is made to keep prices low, it is sometimes necessary to increase prices at short notice. Star Books reserve the right to show new retail prices on covers which may differ from those advertised in the text or elsewhere.